EVENING PRIMROSE

KOPANO MATLWA

Also by Kopano Matlwa

Coconut
Spilt Milk

EVENING PRIMROSE

KOPANO MATLWA

Quercus
New York • London

Quercus

New York • London

© 2016 by Kopano Matlwa
By agreement with Pontas Literary & Film Agency
First published in the United States by Quercus in 2018

ISBN 978-1-63506-032-4

Library of Congress Cataloging-in-Publication Data

Names: Matlwa, Kopano, author.
Title: Evening primrose / Kopano Matlwa.
Description: First edition. | New York : Quercus, 2018.
Identifiers: LCCN 2017045361 (print) | LCCN 2017051543 (ebook) | ISBN 9781635060348 (ebook) | ISBN 9781635060355 (library ebook) | ISBN 9781635060324 (hardcover) | ISBN 9781635060331 (softcover)
Subjects: LCSH: South Africa—Politics and government—1994—Fiction. | Health services accessibility—South Africa—Fiction. | Women physicians—Fiction. | Medical fiction. | BISAC: FICTION / Literary. | FICTION / Cultural Heritage. | FICTION / Medical.
Classification: LCC PR9369.4.M387 (ebook) | LCC PR9369.4.M387 E94 2018 (print) | DDC 823/.92—dc23

LC record available at https://lccn.loc.gov/2017045361

Distributed in the United States and Canada by
Hachette Book Group
1290 Avenue of the Americas
New York, NY 10104

Manufactured in the United States

2 4 6 8 10 9 7 5 3 1

www.quercus.com

For Laone
For Palesa
For Sindiswa
For Shivani
For Khetiwe
For Karabo
For Phindile
For Nomsa
For Oratilwe
For Rudo
For Lebohang
For Mandisa
For Dineo
For Akhona
For Lucy
For Thabitha
For Lerato
For Katlego
For Lulama

For Yolandi
For Funeka
For Kudzai
For Thandeka
For Ilse
For Boitumelo
For Andile
For Gugulethu
For Marea
For Nolitha
For Lesedi
For Tshepiso
For Sibongile
For Hope
For Grace
For you
For me
For our daughters

Part 1

Oh my soul, why are you so downcast within me?

Psalm 43:5

People say that in heaven we'll be happy all the time. We won't cry, we won't feel any pain, we won't be afraid, we'll never worry. Things will be perfect. I once mentioned at Bible Study Group that I found this difficult to imagine. I found the whole idea of it exhausting, like a party that never ends. I'd begun to worry that I wouldn't cope in heaven, that I wouldn't fit in with all the giddy people. But Father Joshua's wife said I should imagine the last time I felt extremely happy and filled with joy. Heaven would be like that moment, just frozen forever.

I tried to think back to graduation, a happy day for me. Bits of the Declaration of Geneva of the World Medical Association came back to me.

I solemnly pledge myself to consecrate my life to the service of humanity . . . The health of my patient will be my first consideration . . .

I'd been practicing those words daily in the weeks leading up to the ceremony, and as we stood there in our gowns saying them in chorus, they fell like notes of high music emanating from my lips.

I remembered waiting for them to call out my name so I could go up to the stage to receive my certificate. There were many of us in the hall, and I was sitting next to people in my class I didn't know very well, the ones I sat next to only during registration, exams, and any other event that required alphabetical ordering. The speeches were long and I couldn't see Ma, so my mind slipped to the fantasies I'd been having for weeks, fantasies about all the things I would do as soon as I graduated.

I pictured myself applying for a clothing account and the lady behind the counter saying "Title, please?" as she typed my details into the system. "Doctor," I'd say. Then I'd open a movie card, and again they'd ask, "Miss or Mrs.?" and I'd say, "Neither, it's Doctor." Then again at the bank, and when booking a flight, and when visiting the dentist. Again and again and again. I'd say it slowly, say it loudly, drag it out, repeat it if I thought they might not have heard the first time. I remember laughing to myself as I sat there between L-ab and L-ij. I couldn't get used to the idea. In just a few minutes I would be a doctor!

A rumor had started that car companies would be waiting at the back of the hall after our graduation ceremony, and brokers waiting to give us mortgages without deposits, as our titles were surety enough. Someone else said there would be financial advisers, too, handing out platinum credit cards with our names already printed on them. I knew all this was nonsense. But I kept turning my head, just in case.

And a certain woman, which had an issue of blood twelve years, and had suffered many things of many physicians, and spent all that she had, and was nothing bettered, but rather grew worse, when she heard of Jesus, came in the press behind, and touched His garment. For she said, if I may touch but His clothes, I shall be whole. And straightway the fountain of her blood was dried up; and she felt in her body that she was healed of that plague. And Jesus, immediately knowing in Himself that virtue had gone out of Him, turned Him about in the press, and said "Who touched My clothes?" And His disciples said unto Him, "Thou seest the multitude thronging Thee and sayest Thou, 'Who touched Me?'" And He looked round about to see her that had done this thing. But the woman fearing and trembling, knowing what was done in her, came and fell down before Him, and told Him all the truth. And He said unto her, "Daughter, thy faith hath made thee whole; go in peace and be whole of thy plague."

Mark 5:25–34

When I first started to bleed, I thought Ma would kill me. I was a naughty child, putting my fingers where I shouldn't, feeling parts of my body I had no business touching. So when, at the Rand Easter Show, I saw a stain on my Tinker Bell knickers, I didn't cry like most little girls would. No, I knew immediately that it was my punishment from God, and hid the evidence. I hid it for days. I collected wads of toilet paper and wrapped them round and round my Woolies full briefs. It was scratchy and uncomfortable, but nothing compared to the discomfort I knew would come with confessing to Ma that I had sinned and was bleeding as a result. That would surely be the end of me. So when I stood on the tips of my tallest toes and pulled the garage door closed on our way to church one Sunday morning, revealing beneath my Scottish Highland–style dress a dark secret that had, until then, remained hidden between my thighs, and Ma asked as I got back into the car what those spots on my glitter tights were, I knew for sure that this was the beginning of my end.

And in some ways it was, because as if in eager response to Ma's question, a floodgate opened within me and blood poured out between my thighs, down my legs, and even onto my Jelly Baby shoes. It continued this way for weeks, easing up for a few days at a time, only to start again with even more intensity, charging past the clots in its way.

I later learned at Sunday School that jugs of serum periodically pouring from one's vagina was no divine punishment at all, but a physiologically necessary and healthy part of a woman's life that should not only be welcomed, but celebrated.

Nonetheless, I prayed relentlessly that the God who had parted the Red Sea and dried it right up for the people He loved might consider blessing me with a season of dry panties.

❖

I remember telling Ma that I wanted it taken out, cut away from me and incinerated in the large chamber at the hospital behind the hill.

She said I was mad.

"*It is* mad!" I screamed.

"It's not mad, Masechaba, it is just unwell."

"Well, *I'm* unwell because of it, Ma."

Ma said I was speaking nonsense, that these were the things women were to endure, and that if it was removed from me I would one day regret being unable to bring life into the world.

Life?

What did I care for bringing life into the world when I couldn't have a life of my own? When I lived hostage to a beast in my pelvis that could split its head at any moment of its choosing, and angrily spill its contents onto the floor at any second of its liking without provocation?

What life did *I* have? Did Ma not care about that?

No, she did not.

❖

I became a loner. Not because I wanted to be alone, but because it was easier for everyone that way. Tshiamo, my brother, was my only friend. The stains didn't seem to bother him as much as they bothered others. Like when Papa bought him a car and he offered to take me for a spin. I was so excited to see Tshiamo excited, I forgot to run into the house and change my tampon and add a second layer to my pad. It was only when we got onto the highway, us foolish at 4:30 p.m. to enter the highway, that I saw the traffic and thought, crap. I tried not to think about it, even when I felt the stickiness between my thighs and knew that the tampon was engorged and the pad saturated and the only way out was through my jeans and onto Tshiamo's new car seat. I tried hard to focus on the Tracy Chapman Tshiamo was singing along to. When we eventually got home, he pretended not to notice, but I knew he had, because I saw him through my bedroom window later with a bucket of soapy water and a sponge in his hand.

❖

At school I always sat at the back of the class, making sure there was never anybody behind me, so that if I messed up my school dress, at least I wouldn't be the last to know.

I was clever and inquisitive at school, and I had no interest in hanging out with the troublemakers who marked out the last row of desks as their own. But I knew that if I was to maintain a seat for myself far from the suspicious eyes of the cruelest girls, I had to be as badass as the best of them.

❖

You learn some tricks as you go. Dark clothing, ski pants under my school tunic, a cheap, thick, no-name brand pad under the Always Infinity to absorb the inevitable overflow. I was never without a tampon in my bra, so that if I had to dash to the bathroom in a crowd, I didn't have to bend over and scrabble through my schoolbag first. Ballet? Forget it. Synchronized swimming? Are you crazy? Gymnastics? Not even if I was paid. Netball? Risky. Running? Sometimes.

No parties. No sleepovers. Ma wanted none of the humiliation that would come with a phone call from another parent to advise that her daughter had bled through the sheets and onto the mattress. She pretended it didn't bother her, but I knew she was just as embarrassed and perplexed by the aggression of her daughter's young womb as everybody else was.

She would say things like, "It's because you eat too much cheese! That's why you bleed the way you do," or "Those tampons you use, they're unnatural. They keep the dirt from coming out freely."

It made me angry when she said things like that, because she knew just as well as I did that those old wives' tales were nonsense. No amount of cheese could explain my dysfunctional uterine bleeding and the accompanying dizziness, fainting spells, and galloping heartbeat that didn't have much to gallop about. She knew that if it was as simple as letting the so-called "dirt" flow out freely, I'd be walking around with no pad or paper, not even a tanga or high-cuts, just bare for all the world to see, if that was what it would take to stop the madness that came from within.

❖

I was always light-headed, always fainting, my heart always racing in my chest at high speed. In and out of the hospital I went, transfusion after transfusion, pill after pill, patch after patch, injection after injection.

❖

Eventually the bleeding eased up, in fact almost stopped altogether, bar a little bit of spotting on the occasional month. I can't remember how or the specific day. It may have been the endometrial ablation that finally did it. I was too young to understand, but I remember Ma telling Aunty Petunia that the doctors had said that short of a hysterectomy, the only thing that might work was to burn the lining of the womb.

"Let them burn it, Ma!" I remember crying.

She had shouted at me to be quiet. But I think after I fainted into Rakgadi Tebogo's pool at Dineo's traditional wedding, Ma stopped caring about the life I'd never be able to bring into the world and started worrying more about the life she'd brought into it.

❖

But I didn't trust, and continued to carry around pads, tampons, toilet paper, wipes, and black panties wherever I went. When clutch purses were in vogue, I watched enviously as pretty girls walked around the mall with a couple of notes and a lip gloss in the glittering pouches in their hands. But I knew better than to let my guard down. The beast was only sleeping, and could wake at any moment.

So on job-shadow day, when I saw (through the narrow space between the oversized surgical cap, mask, and goggles they insisted I wear) a neurosurgeon climb onto the operating table and let his colleague release the pinched nerve from his back that had been troubling him all morning, I knew immediately that it was a message from God, and that it was in this very manner that I would get the abhorrent organ cut out of me and destroyed, once and for all.

When Ma asked me later that evening how the day had gone, I told her it had been nothing short of marvelous, and that I was 120 percent sure that a medical doctor was what I wanted to be. She smiled when she heard me say that. It was a good profession, she said, and she had no doubt I'd make a great physician who would one day help a lot of people.

I hadn't thought about the people until she mentioned them. At that moment I decided it was unwise to tell her that I only wanted to become a doctor so I could make a friend at medical school who'd be willing to do the hysterectomy that all the doctors we'd seen so far had refused to perform.

But that was all a very long time ago, and by the time the title was mine, these childish musings were all but forgotten.

Why O Lord do you reject me and hide your face from me? From my youth I have been afflicted and close to death; I have suffered your terrors and am in despair. Your wrath has swept over me; your terrors have destroyed me. All day long they surround me like a flood; they have completely engulfed me. You have taken my companions and loved ones from me; the darkness is my closest friend.

Psalm 88:14–18

Father Joshua wasted no time after my graduation. Within weeks of my receiving my medical practitioner's license from the Health Professionals Council of South Africa, he asked me to speak to the youth about careers. He said young people needed to be encouraged. Our people didn't value education anymore, he lamented, and maybe if they saw someone like me doing well, they might be inspired.

I told him I'd love to. But I was lying, of course. I hated public speaking, and I really didn't have much to say. As far as I was concerned, if you're clever, you become a doctor. Government contracts finish, and sometimes they don't pay, and sometimes you get arrested. But if you study, it stays with you for life.

Tshiamo painted pain, but it made him think too many deep thoughts, so he hanged himself on a tree. Papa got government contracts, but they reshuffled the cabinet and brought in people he didn't know. There were irregularities that required a sacrificial lamb, so he was in the newspapers and is now with Gogo, in her back room, drinking the days that remain away. As for me, Ma found an admin job in government. She worked at the Department of Health so she could get me a bursary, which made it easy. There were not a million things I could choose from, anyhow. Seriti University was close to home, and Botshelo Hospital always needed intern doctors.

But I couldn't say no to Father Joshua. I couldn't come across as too self-important to spend some time with the youth. So I wrote the stories I knew they wanted to hear, and emailed them to Tshiamo for his comments.

Of course I didn't expect a response. I'm not crazy. Nor was I ever in denial. But people mourn differently, and I was entitled to mourn whichever way I saw fit. The people at Gmail didn't seem to mind. They kept on delivering my emails to Tshiamo just like they'd always done. Not like Ma, or Malome Softly, or Gogo and everyone else, who would have minded a lot and were nothing like they'd always been.

Of course I knew Tshiamo was dead. There was no shortage of reminders. But what is knowing, anyway? I've known ever since I've had a thinking mind that I would one day die, but does that mean I wake up every morning preoccupied with it? Of course not. That would be absurd. I know Tshiamo's dead, thank you very much. Thank you for being so concerned that I'm unaware of the worst thing that's ever happened in my life. Thank you, you're all so terribly kind. But can I choose to forget for just a moment? Would that be okay with you? Just like I choose to forget

that the world is evil and our government corrupt and the
West forever plotting our demise?

Can I please continue giving R20 notes to the man sitting
outside Checkers and continue praying for the homeless and
the downtrodden? And, if it's no inconvenience to you, can I
please continue sending emails to my dead brother who was
my only friend, the only person who cared to see me, who
cared to give me of his time and interest and humor? Can
I pretend he will be back from his art workshop at 6 p.m.
with a smile and an empty lunch bag in his hand? Is that
okay with you, world?

Might I be left alone in peace to send smiley faces and
photographs to my dead brother, who I miss more than anything in the entire universe, whose death left a hole in me so
big I thought I might slip and fall through it?

No, it is not okay with the world. There is nothing that
bothers the world more. So I stopped. Because long after
Malome Softly stepped into Tshiamo's grave and poured
soil over his head; long after Aunty Petunia grabbed my arm
and forced me to go and look at his face in the casket against
my will, like I was a child, like she was a somebody in our
lives; long after people stopped coming to visit us, drinking all the tea and finishing the last bucket of scones; long
after our neighbors forgot that we were mourning and that
they needed to be nice to us, Malome Softly's girlfriend,
who I thought was my friend, spotted my *Sent* mailbox as I
was scrolling through my phone, and went to tell Ma that

I was communicating with my dead brother, and she was worried I was practicing witchcraft. I had no choice then but to stop sending emails to Tshiamo and to instead write everything in this stupid journal that is read by no one but God. When He can find the time.

Since my people are crushed, I am crushed; I mourn, and horror grips me.

Is there no balm in Gilead? Is there no physician there?

Why then is there no healing for the wound of my people?

Jeremiah 8:21–22

When we were little, Tshiamo and I always used to play "Doctor Doctor." He thought it was dumb, but he knew how much I enjoyed the game, so he went along with it. Not always, though, not on his down days. It wasn't like he was a saint or anything. Sometimes I'd have to beg him for hours, and promise to leave him alone for the rest of the day if he agreed to play with me for just a little bit. And I really did mean a little bit. Everything was already set up, the patients were on the table, I was scrubbed up, the drugs were drawn and labeled and the instruments ready. I just needed a surgical nurse to assist me.

Tshiamo would look at me in disgust as he walked into my room filled with teddy bears whose throats had been slit, yellow stuffing pouring out of them. I'd smile and tell him not to panic, I was going to save them. And I did. I always saved them.

❖

I remember first learning about cells in Grade 10 Biology. Mrs. McCartney described them like little factories in our bodies—no, like cities with many factories inside them. She said there were billions of them all packed tightly together.

I tried to imagine them, to picture all that activity inside of me. I remember being struck by how much I still had to learn, and wondering if I would ever fully understand the functioning of the human body.

Ma said I worried too much. She reminded me of how concerned I was in Grade 1 that I'd never be able to read. I laughed when she said that. It still amazes me, though, how we go from looking at apples and cats on a big colorful chart to memorizing the names of the blood vessels of the heart to inserting a central venous pressure line into a patient's neck. I guess this ability we all have—to go from looking at street signs and roundabouts in a learner's permit study book to overtaking trucks on the highway—makes us a little reckless when it comes to what we think we're capable of achieving.

I see now that there was actually a lot of luck in my getting to this point, and perhaps a lot of unseen effort by those around me. Like the exam study guides that slowly filled my bedroom and the extra lessons Ma insisted Papa pay for. So when I saw green peas come out of bed A3's neck, I knew my luck had run out.

Dr. Voel-Vfamba said that is how we learn, that she was going to die anyway and that I shouldn't feel bad.

❖

Patients die all the time. Nobody expects you to save all of them all the time. We do what we can. And with our crumbling health system, our staff shortages, our social challenges, well, what can people really expect? We do what we can. This is the mantra I sing to myself, day and night, night and day. I sing it to others, they sing it to me.

"We do what we can."

"We do what we can."

They come to hospital so late anyway, what can you do really? They are irresponsible, many of them. They know better, but our people refuse to take responsibility for their own health. And then it's the government, the district, the minister, the president.

"We do what we can."

"We do what we can."

Again and again, I sing the words, repeat the speech, sometimes silently, sometimes violently. But when the (irresponsible?) mother of the (now dead) baby is running down the corridor, security behind her, Sister Agnes drawing up Valium, patients watching from their beds, mouths agape, and it's your call, your shift, your patient, your incident, another death on your watch, the mantra does not work. The Gini coefficients, the shrinking economy, the legacy of apartheid, the unachieved Millennium Development Goals and human resource constraints, these are all disloyal friends who abandon you to face your conscience alone. You kill the patients alone. You kill them alone.

❖

Sometimes you turn your car around, call the referral hospital again. Maybe you will find bed A3 an ICU bed if you call just one more time. Sometimes you leave with packets of donor blood in your pockets that you forgot to drop off at the emergency department on your way out. Sometimes you accept a lift home, forgetting that you had driven in that morning.

❖

You learn a lot in the dead of the night: that if you cry while you are peeing, and hang your head between your legs, the tears collect in your eyelashes, so that when you walk back into the ward, there are no lines down your face but stars before your eyes.

❖

There is also a lot of good. Like the credit you get. That's always good. And those moments when people try to explain medical stuff to you, like at the travel clinic, only to pick up the patient information card and flush with embarrassment at the "Dr." beside your name. All of that is good. Letters in the post are always nice. Your electronic signature, that's also nice, all of that is good. But there's a lot of bad. Like when your tongue twists in your mouth and your neck turns round and round and round, making you want to scream but only knotting tighter each time you try. That sucks. And having to go back every day. That really sucks.

I tell Ma of the many horrific things our people overcome daily that go undocumented. I tell her that somebody must list them, all the bad things that are happening to them, to me, to us. Somebody needs to write them down.

Ma says I must leave them there, the patients. I must walk in their shoes, but try not to bring their shoes home. So I leave them there, stuck between the soiled sheets and the sandwich hidden for the day an appetite returns, between toilets caked in shit and the soap dispenser that only worked once, the day the minister came to visit. But I fail at walking in their shoes. They have no shoes, Ma. How can I walk in their shoes when they have no shoes?

❖

The people at Bible Study advise me to pray to Jesus for them. They ask for their names. They will email them around the church and the congregation will pray for them. They ask and they ask and they ask. "What are their names? We will pray to Jesus for them," they insist. Names? Are these people stupid? How do they expect me to remember the names of hundreds of people crammed into a ward designed for a couple of dozen? How do they expect me to distinguish individuals among a sea of dying arms and mangled bodies glued to mangled beds?

And besides, Jesus wouldn't get it. Jesus never failed at anything. He never did a thing wrong. That's the fundamental difference. Having to live with failure will always set us apart from the Son of God. Having to live with the shame of not being better, not being courageous, not being great.

❖

Professor Siyatula didn't warn us about any of this. When we were walking behind him on those grand ward rounds, hanging onto every word he spoke, fingers clutching at the hem of his garment, he, the only black specialist in a white institution, didn't warn us about the suffering, the helplessness, the fear, the contempt that awaited us. There were no clues, no hints about just how bad things were going to be. We were doctors, *mos*. Well paid, well heeled. Was there anything we couldn't handle?

❖

There are heroes. The ones with a skip in their step, the strange ones that don't seem to need sleep, who walk around with irritating grins on their faces. But they are a minority. Most are broken and tired people, with bonds and university loans needing to be paid, so they stay on, doing what they can. I like to think I'm somewhere in the middle of that, but probably more broken than a hero.

❖

Were I at my best I could be great. The Charlotte Maxeke, Hamilton Naki, William Anderson Soga kind of great. But I am not at my best. I am tired. I have a ward full of patients and no anti-nausea medication I can safely take without developing extrapyramidal side effects, so I must chew gum through my six weeks of post-exposure prophylaxis and just suck it up. I have urine on my last pair of clean scrubs, because Dr. Voel-Vfamba asked me to drain a urine catheter bag and the valve got stuck, drenching me and my notes with body fluid. I cannot be great, even if I want to be.

❖

"Watch one, do one, teach one." How many people did we kill monthly, weekly, daily, all in the name of learning? "Watch one, do one, teach one."

I can't tell you the number of times I heard those words, and how I hated them. Because I was never that kind of junior intern. I had to watch a million before I could do one, and even then I was likely to botch that one and the next and the one after, so that I had to be taught it all over again. Does it make me a bad doctor that I'm not a cowboy? That I can't waltz into a ward, grab a pair of sterile gloves, tear them open with my teeth and plunge a central line into Mrs. Mazibuko's neck? She died, you know. I couldn't sleep for days. I remember me and Dr. Voel-Vfamba standing on a stool, him trying to hold her still and me pushing the long needle into her neck. Maybe she didn't die from that. The peas that followed made no sense. Maybe it wasn't our fault. The central venous pressure line was a last-ditch attempt anyway. She was long on her way. But something tells me that we pushed her over the edge.

Murderers, all of us. Murderers.

That's why I chewed so many Xanax. You have to be numb. How else are you to survive it all? She looked just like Rakgadi Juice. And worse, she trusted me. I'm the one who convinced her to sign the consent form. To Dr. Voel-Vfamba, she was bed A3, the cardiac failure in bed A3. It was my job to protect her from him, from all of them, all those vultures, those third-year students with their logbooks desperate for signatures, signatures at any cost. I should have protected her from the registrars who sought nothing else but to clear the ward so they could study for their exams, from the specialists with papers to write. *"A rare case of drug-induced cardiomyopathy in an elderly black female."* But I didn't save her. Instead I aided and abetted, facilitated, won her over—and then handed her over. And now she's dead.

❖

I want to cry, but it takes too much time, too much energy. I want to run away, to escape, but to where?

Escaping requires planning, thinking, organizing. I feel like I am drowning in myself. Is that possible? To drown in the blood coursing through your own veins? I feel like the air in my lungs is choking me. Like there is a small me inside the big me that is sinking, struggling. Somewhere deep inside of me there is a thing in need of saving. Something in there is in trouble. It is screaming, it is gasping, it is dying.

❖

Sister Agnes was furious at us. She didn't think the procedure was necessary, and had said a number of times that Mrs. Mazibuko should be discharged and allowed to go home and spend her last days with her family. But the specialists had insisted. What choice did we have? I heard Sister Agnes later say to one of the matrons that these were the kinds of things that made her want to take her retirement package and go watch her grandchildren play at her feet.

"They are children. They think like children and they behave like children. They may know books, but nothing else. I'm sure some of them haven't even started menstruating yet."

❖

I blame the barrel. It's not me. The barrel was rotten to begin with, before I got into it. I'm a good apple, really I am. The barrel made me rotten, rotten to the core.

❖

Who said we had to enjoy caring for the ill? I mean, one ought to do it, it's morally right to do it, but do you have an obligation to enjoy it? Would it make you a bad person if you said you detested it? Hated every minute of it? Did it, but deplored it?

❖

Sometimes I want to feel stuff. I'm doing a resuscitation and I know I should feel something, but I don't know how to anymore. There's something in me that's blocked, that's stuck. There's a weight on my chest, and I try to breathe it off, but I can't. So when the patients die, I am relieved. I tell myself it's better for them to die. They're suffering, they're in pain. I try to justify it. I'm tired, Lord. I'm tired of seeing them every day, tired of seeing their faces. I'm tired of being reminded of how little I can do. I'm tired of the drips that keep coming out. I'm tired of seeing them eat their poo and drink their pee. I'm tired of seeing them go mad. I'm tired of watching their families come every day and look to me for answers I cannot give them. I'm tired of working with people who don't care, who are dead like me. I can't even remember why I did this in the first place, why I was so foolish to think that being a doctor, that six years at medical school, would bring me happiness. All it's brought me is pain and confusion.

❖

I don't know how I expected "doing good" to feel. But I didn't think it would be like this. There's no magic, no divine enlightenment. It's as hard as doing bad. You're just as tired, just as scared, just as disillusioned, just as broken. I thought there was supposed to be some sort of anointing, some filling of the Holy Spirit, some peace that would come with doing God's work. But there's none of that.

❖

When Jesus told the Twelve that he knew one of them was going to betray him, was he hoping that once that one realized he knew, he would change his ways and repent from his evil? And if not, if Jesus knew it was all inevitable, how unfair to Judas that he had no way out, that he was predestined to be forever known as the traitor of the Son of God.

❖

Why is this place so broken? Why did You let it get so
bad? Why don't You do something about it? I don't want to
be a part of it, of this. I hate it here. I can't be happy. You
can't ask me to be happy in this. One has to be crazy to be
happy in this. I'm only a human being, I'm not a god. I'm
not Jesus. I'm not You. Why do You ask so much of me?

I do not understand what I do. For what I want to do, I do not do, but what I hate I do.

Romans 7:15

Paradoxically, I'd felt sorry for myself when the heavy bleeding stopped. It had been the thorn in my flesh, the burden that was my very own, sorry load to bear. Even though there was never a place I could go without a packet of pads and a box of tampons, they'd become my trusted companions, my loyal childhood friends. So when the crazy bleeding stopped, I found myself without a reason not to put on a white summer dress and go out into the world. There was no excuse for not running, not dancing, not flying. But I was afraid. What if the wings came loose and the panty liner slipped down the side of my leg, and I fell? What if, while having so much fun, I forgot to be careful, forgot to check?

But being with Nyasha gave me courage. She was so brave, so funny, so unapologetic. Around her nothing seemed impossible. Her womb was completely dried up because she'd had a Mirena put into her uterus as soon as she started working. As she explained, she wanted none of that nonsense getting in her way.

Ma didn't like her, of course.

"These *kwere-kweres*, Masechaba, they'll use their black magic to steal all your intelligence, your whole future. Everything you've worked so hard for will be gone, and you'll be left with the nothing they arrived in this country with."

So I moved out of the house.

Nyasha and I rented a flat close to the hospital. Often we'd drive together to work if neither of us were on call. It was something I was always going to do anyway, I just hadn't yet found anyone I felt comfortable sharing a place with. You can't live under your mother's roof forever, and anyway, it's not like I was far away. A person needs space. Tshiamo would probably criticize me for leaving Ma alone in that big house, but what right does he have to criticize me? People who have no respect for life have no right telling others how to live theirs.

❖

I met Nyasha at a minor car accident scene. I'd seen her before at work, on the wards. I noticed her because she had beautiful, jet-black dreadlocks and a quiet confidence that was fearsome to behold. She was a medical officer in the Obstetrics & Gynecology Department, waiting for a specialist training post. However, it was well known in the hospital that if it wasn't for her foreign nationality, she would already be a consultant obstetrician-gynecologist, because she was a surgeon extraordinaire.

I watched her one night, joking with a mother who was a heartbeat away from losing a perfectly healthy baby. The baby's umbilical cord had slipped out of the woman's vagina during labor, and Nyasha stood for four hours with a damp cloth in that bloody cavity, keeping the cord moist until an operating room opened up and the obstetrician had arrived on the premises. All the while she was laughing, Red Bull in one hand, the baby's life in the other. I knew then that I wanted her as my friend, and that I'd do whatever it took to make sure she was in my life.

I tried to make conversation with her on the nights we were on call together. She was polite enough, but always busy. Busy saving lives while us interns fumbled along. Then one morning as I drove to work, I noticed her driving in front of me, and it occurred to me that this might be my only chance. I drove alongside her, in front of her, and then finally let her pass me again. At the hospital there was never time to talk. There was no excuse for long conversations that might end up in a friendship, no environment conducive enough to finding out more about this beautiful woman with piercing brown eyes. So as the traffic light changed from green to yellow and then to red, I pushed hard on the accelerator and drove into her.

Tshiamo would be horrified.

"The lengths you'll go to, Masechaba!"

But nobody got hurt. I knew she wouldn't get hurt. I would never hurt her. Not like Tshiamo, who paid no mind to how he might hurt us.

He knew better than to leave a note, that foolish boy. Because I wouldn't have read it, anyway. I would have torn it to shreds and set it alight. He's full of nonsense,

Tshiamo. We're all going through shit. Who the hell does he think he is?

❖

Nyasha doesn't say much about Zimbabwe. I don't ask too many questions, in case I offend her or expose my ignorance. All I know is that her mother is a nurse in Bristol. I don't know if there's a father, and I've never heard her speak of siblings, although she did mention she has a cousin specializing as an ENT surgeon in the US.

I feel bad about how our country treats them. We should know better, what with apartheid and all. Nyasha is quite fair skinned, and actually looks South African, so you wouldn't even know she was foreign until you speak to her.

Sometimes she upsets me, though. She speaks like an authority on what we South Africans should and should not do, as if she has some sort of expertise. Just the other day she came home upset about a white patient she'd just admitted, who asked if there was a girl who could help him carry his bags to the ward. Nyasha was outraged by his use of the word "girl" and went off on a tirade about how arrogant white South Africans are. I responded that she needed to be the bigger person in those kinds of situations. She was the doctor, and he was a patient in pain who didn't know what he meant.

She called me an idiot. That's why we South Africans will continue to live under the illusion of freedom, she said, unaware of how we remain captive to white supremacy.

I told her she needed to surrender all her anger to You. I said I'd never had a racist experience at work and that the people there are actually quite nice, if you bother to get to know them. Everyone is nice, once you get to know them.

She gave me one of her looks.

I'm not going to let her get to me. She's always looking for drama where there isn't any. Sometimes I want to tell her to go back to her own country and fix her own problems and stop meddling in ours. But I'd never say that. It's not a nice thing to say. I was blessed to be born in South Africa. It's not her fault that she wasn't. Those who have should give to those who don't have.

❖

We seem to fight a lot these days, Nyasha and I. Maybe it's me. I'm so tired all the time, tired and irritable. I can't remember the last time we had a good weekend. Was it as far back as when we brought home all the leftover champagne from the departmental Christmas party? We stayed up watching movies, laughing, then stuffed our faces with cheese samosas, piri-piri potato wedges, and prince prawns. I'm surprised we didn't vomit. We were so happy. We couldn't believe we'd both managed to avoid being on call that weekend, the entire weekend! Nyasha said it felt like the sleepover she'd never had. When she moved to South Africa as a teenager, her mother forbade her from sleeping at other girls' houses in case she got molested. She didn't trust anybody in this crazy country. I laughed, and called her xenophobic. She laughed, too, and said that South Africans thought they owned xenophobia. It was a happy day. A happy weekend.

I'd never been allowed a sleepover either, so it meant a lot to me, too, although I didn't say it. At home there were always large maroon towels on my bed. Hard towels, not soft, new ones, because that would just be a waste. Hard, dark towels that could keep a secret.

❖

On call, last night, the paramedics brought in this white lady at about 1:30 a.m. She was at home with her boyfriend when four men broke into their flat, raped her, shot her in the head, and ransacked the house. I didn't get the full story because the specialist doctor on call was panicked and sent us all running around. I was told to take femoral blood and get it to the blood bank. When I came back the surgical team was preparing her to operate. She was fully conscious and speaking despite the shot to her head, which was weird. On my way to the blood bank I heard one of the paramedics telling a nurse that the police had found blood splattered across her living room walls and her boyfriend had died at the scene, but she hadn't been told yet.

When I went back to bed after taking the emergency blood to the operating room, I pictured those walls.

I told Nyasha the story this morning when I got home. The white interns were saying in the morning meeting that this was the reason they were taking the UK PLAB and US MLE exams and getting out of the country.

"Let them go," is what she had to say. "Our people are just rag dolls for them to perfect their clinical skills for the white people they'll be serving in the private sector. Let them go."

You know *mos* Nyasha, Lord.

❖

Do you ever get that feeling that this is me and that is them? That I am me, and you are you, and that we are separate? That I am here, and you are there? That this is my life and that is yours? That these are my thoughts and you have your own, and they are apart from mine?

❖

I asked Nyasha if being a doctor ever felt scary for her. Did she sometimes feel like she couldn't breathe? Like there was a large invisible boulder on her chest?

I shouldn't have bothered, because instead of the empathy I was hoping for, I got a scolding instead.

"Stop talking nonsense, Chaba! Your problem is you spend too much time with those white intcrns. They're getting into your head. Can't breathe? Why can't you breathe? Do you have TB? Are your airways clogged with pneumocystis pneumonia? No? Then why can't you breathe?"

❖

Tomorrow I'm going to wake up early and get to the hospital on time. I'm going to be in the lab first thing in the morning and make sure I have all the patients' results before the ward round. I'm going to check their temperatures myself if the nurses haven't done them yet. I'm going to stop others discharging them before they're well enough to go home. I'm going to ask them how they feel, instead of making it up.

It probably won't change anything. I'll probably be back in this same empty place by lunchtime. No, by half past eight. But I'm going to try, anyway. I'm going to wake up early and make a list of all the things I need to do for the day. I'm going to read around every patient's condition so I can be of some help to them. Maybe I'll find something clever in those scientific journals. Maybe I'll find a way to save some of them. I'm going to be different. I'm going to stay on longer in the afternoons and I'm going to offer to help the other doctors with their work when I'm done with mine. And I'm going to remember to pray.

❖

Great news, Lord. I found out from Nyasha that there are rumors that the nurses are going on strike. That means no elective surgeries, because there'll be no nurses to assist. Which means Thursday afternoons are free. This has to be a miracle! Thank you! Thank you! Thank you!

My God, my God, why have You abandoned me? I have cried desperately for help, but still it does not come. During the day I call to You, my God, but You do not answer; I call at night, but get no rest. But You are enthroned as the Holy One, the One whom Israel praises. Our ancestors put their trust in You; they trusted You and You saved them. They called to You and escaped from danger; they trusted You and were not disappointed.

But I am no longer a human being; I am a worm, despised and scorned by everyone! All who see me jeer at me; they stick out their tongues and shake their heads. "You relied on the Lord," they say. "Why doesn't He save you? If the Lord likes you, why doesn't He help you?"

Psalm 22:1–8

I certified two patients dead this morning. I felt nothing. I tried forcing myself to pause, to stop, to acknowledge. But nothing came. I even tried doing the sign of the cross, but nothing stirred within me.

Maybe I'm just PMS-ing.

❖

Next month I start my Obstetrics & Gynecology rotation with a call. I feel nothing but dread for the hours I will be spending sucking dead babies out of little girls' vaginas. I hate the Obstetrics & Gynecology staff. I hate the environment, I hate the smells. The nurses there are mean and cruel, especially to the foreign patients. They call them dirt. They shout at them for coming in the middle of the night without antenatal books. They ask them why they fill up our wards. They look at the scabs on their legs, smack their lips, and remark, "You see this one? You can tell she jumped the border only just yesterday."

They scrunch up their noses when they examine them. They laugh at their names. They speak to them in Sesotho, isiXhosa, isiZulu, even though they know they can't understand.

And then there's me, standing there, smiling sheepishly. "Don't worry, they're just joking," I try to reassure them when I'm alone with them in the examination room. I can see in their eyes that they know I'm lying. So I say nothing more.

I'm afraid of the Obstetrics & Gynecology nurses. If I reprimand them I'll create hell for myself in that department for the duration of my rotation. And possibly beyond. So instead of telling them that what they're doing is wrong, and possibly illegal, I do nothing.

I'm a coward. If this were apartheid, I'd be one of those quiet white people who just stood by and watched it happen.

❖

I tell Ma about the kidney dish that still has *Slegs Blankes* engraved into it, that the nurses keep for foreign patients. I tell her how appalling it is that we've become the very thing we fought so long and hard to destroy. Ma says she doesn't blame the nurses. She's watched their movies, and foreigners can hide their magic in anything.

❖

What is it inside of us that makes us so evil? And how do we become better? Why are we capable of so much harm and badness? How do we change? And stay changed?

❖

Nyasha says her group of new intern doctors all have weaves. Twelve girls as black as night, with mops of plastic on their heads. She is annoyed.

"Stupid girls. Book smart, but stupid. They can tell you the nerve that innervates the stapedius muscle, but they can't see the foolishness in walking around with heaps of self-hatred on their heads."

She wants me to get involved.

"Why don't you tell them, Chaba? These are your sisters, your South African sisters. Maybe if you speak to them, you can put some sense into their heads."

I say nothing, so she continues. "We know we hate ourselves as black people. That we know. But now we're exposing ourselves to white people, too. Now we are exposing this dark stain of self-hatred on our race. We're giving them evidence that we are indeed a foolish, self-loathing people. A thing to be pitied. How much do those weaves cost? These girls have only been working a few months and already they're enriching the industries that strive to oppress us instead of building our communities."

Her tirade continues, and she seems not bothered by my obvious disinterest.

"Now I must keep these dreadlocks, even though they wear my head down, even though I've grown tired of them, because one of us, some of us, must have pride. We can't all walk around like mad people. If aliens were to come from Mars, what would they make of us, Chaba?"

Nyasha wants to fight, fight, fight. She hates white people and blames them for everything. Maybe she's right, maybe they are to blame. But it is what it is. What's happened has happened. We can't go back, and we certainly can't change who we are to try to avenge the past. She says we black South Africans are too nice, too accommodating, too soft. "Weak" and "pathetic" are the words she uses to describe us.

"We need to stop bending over backward, breaking our backs to make them feel comfortable, welcome, safe. Put a white man in charge and he'll only serve his own interests."

Maybe, Nyasha, maybe that's true, but maybe it isn't. And maybe, Nyasha, we need to remember that this world is fallen. There are wars we will never win, and maybe the end game is not to triumph over fleeting kingdoms in this life, but to conquer the battle for eternity.

Of course she scoffs when I say things like that.

"Why does your god make it so hard for us to love him, Chaba? Why play these games? Create this world, bring us here, only to watch us suffer? Why does he hide? Is he a coward? Why doesn't he come out here and see the mess he's made, come see how his creation is doing?"

I'm no good at arguing. I get too overwhelmed and my mind goes blank, so I say nothing.

❖

Ma insists that my friendship with Nyasha will only result
in pain. She insists that foreigners are crafty, and that Nyasha is only being my friend to steal all my knowledge and
overtake me. This is what foreigners like to do, she says.
They come to our country to take from us all the things we
fought for.

I've given up trying to reason with Ma. When I go home
on weekends she makes me take off my clothes at the door;
she doesn't want me coming into the house with Nyasha's
charms and black magic. It's her way of getting back at me
for leaving her and moving in with Nyasha.

If only they knew how similar they were, how much they
have in common. They both want me to hate white people, but
I don't want to. I don't want to hate foreigners, either. I don't
want to hate anybody. It's tiring. I'm already so tired from
work. It's much more than I can deal with at the moment.

But they constantly remind me that I must. They retell
old stories of deceit, of conniving, of looting, and then
share new ones. I don't want to disappoint them, make
them worry that I'm unfocused, that I've dropped the ball.
So I often just nod in agreement and hope they'll stop. But
this ball is too heavy to carry. It hurts my arms, and with it
in my hands I cannot do anything else.

❖

So I don't tell Nyasha what I did with François at the Christmas party. And when he walks past me in the doctors' parking lot and smiles, she's immediately annoyed and goes off on one of her tirades.

"White men think they can just smile at a black woman and she'll oblige. They think we should be flattered that they even see us. No, not just flattered, honored. It makes me sick. Even the morbidly obese ones, who could never summon the courage to approach one of their own, think we'll just drop our panties at the sight of their skin."

I pretend not to hear, mumble that I have pre-op bloods to take before the morning ward round, and rush off.

❖

Nyasha is a lone wolf at work. I never see her in the doctors' canteen. She always eats on the run. She's polite with the staff, but she doesn't care much for small talk. I don't even bother asking her to have lunch with me. I know there'll be an excuse. I recently learned that there are other friends, a writing group that meets weekly, where she goes to share her poetry with others. I learned about the group—and the other friends—not because she's ever cared to tell me, but from the Post-its on her wall, the makeup on a Wednesday morning, and the reminder on the fridge. I don't care that she's never invited me along. I wouldn't want to go, anyway. Who still meets to recite poetry anyway? That's so '90s. Maybe it's a Zimbabwean thing. Who knows?

❖

There's nothing worse than having a good dream disrupted. You can't get back into it. I dreamed François and I were on a quad bike, me nestled cozily into his crotch as he directed us through hills of mud. I was in a bikini, a white bikini, unconcerned that blood might come spilling between my legs and ruin everything. But the phone rang twice, then three times, then nonstop, so I picked it up. I knew as soon as I heard Ma's voice on the other end, rambling about Aunty Petunia not inviting her to Seipati's *magadi*, that I should never have answered, and that sleep and my dream were irretrievably gone and I'd have to listen to Ma for at least another ten minutes before I could make up an excuse to get off the phone.

❖

I hate mornings because that's where all the sadness waits. From the ringing of my alarm clock to the fighting with my hair to being late anyway, despite how hard I try to prepare in advance. My car is a casket that daily carries me to my death. I ask myself over and over if I shouldn't just leave, start over, go back to the beginning, but then the voices in my head begin to get loud.

"What will you do if you quit?"

"You're no good at anything else."

"Do you want to waste six years of your life?"

I try to tell them I'm not good at this anyway, that I'd rather waste six years of my life than the lives I can't help. But they don't want to listen.

❖

Sometimes I see things out of the corner of my eye. The red washing basket on the floor is a squatting man in a red hoodie, trying hard not to be seen. Sometimes a fork rises from the pile on the dish rack. When I flick my head around to catch it, it lies motionless, cold and lifeless. I ignore these cracks in my psyche the way a smoker ignores the occasional speck of blood in his sputum. I dare not ask the obvious. Am I going mad?

If my mind were to fall apart, what would become of me? Would I be just another has-been lying numb and drugged in the female psychiatric ward watching medical students poke around in my file?

❖

I feel like I'm on a bus hurtling along the highway at 150 miles an hour. I'm not clear where we're headed and fear I'll hate it when I get there. The people on the bus aren't

my friends. The driver doesn't hear my pleas to stop.
Nobody does, and I'm not sure if I'm only pleading inside
my head. I can't get up. I have to stay seated with my
seat belt strapped. To get up and remove it is a criminal
offense, the driver says. I stare at the stickers on the windows. *Emergency Exit, Break Glass. Emergency Hammer
Under Rack, Break Glass.* The stickers are everywhere.
Have they been put there for me? Perhaps they're trying to help me. Perhaps they know. But what is a rack,
and how do I get beneath it? And if I get the hammer in
my hand, how long will I have to break the window and
escape before I'm charged with the crime of unstrapping
my seat belt?

❖

Maybe I'm depressed. I don't know. Regardless, I'm not
going onto Prozac. The last thing I need is to put on weight.
Then I'll be even more depressed.

I don't know who I am anymore. I don't know what
defines me. I feel like a failure. I'm not a saint, I'm not like
Mother Teresa, Florence Nightingale, Albertina Sisulu.
I'm not like those people. I don't know how to be like
them. I don't know how to wake up every day and have
patients cough MDR-TB into my face, and not mind. I
mind. I want to be some kind of hero, but I don't have it
in me. I'm not that, I don't know how to be that. I wish

I was. I wish I could hold their shit in my hands and love them. But I can't.

I hate them.

❖

Why am I so bad? Why did You make me this way? I want to be different, better, kinder, but I don't know how.

❖

Jesus? Do You see me?

❖

I wish You wouldn't hide Yourself from me.

❖

On the way to work this morning, I asked Nyasha if she ever wishes certain people would die. Yes, she said, she often hopes many of these politicians would die, all these old men ruining our continent. She doesn't understand why they've lived so long. She doubts they lead healthy lives. They can't possibly be compliant with their diabetic medications and their antihypertensives. She's hoping they'll die soon. By 2025 most of them will be dead, she estimates, and then we can take over the continent and right all their wrongs. Fix the mess. Take Africa to its rightful place on the world stage. She started going off on a tangent about why it's so important for young people to start preparing for that future, to stop wasting time on Twitter and Facebook and start preparing to rebuild the continent. She quoted someone famous, saying it would be a shame if our moment to act arrived and we were caught unprepared.

You know *mos* Nyasha, Lord.

I asked her if she ever wished certain patients would die.

She looked at me funny and said no. She said nothing more all the rest of the way to work.

❖

I know this is no way for a human being, a good human being, to think, Lord. I would never say these things out loud, and I swear not to write this kind of thing anymore. But you know Noluthando, that stage-four lady with cervical cancer, who's bed bound and has fistulas coming out of everywhere? Well, wouldn't it be better if You took her, Lord? Wouldn't it be better if she died? I have to put up a drip in her daily, Lord.

She's so confused now, she takes her drip out every day. She's not eating, doesn't speak much, and we can't get hold of her family. What's the point, really? Aren't we just causing her even more pain and distress than she needs? And

Betty. To be honest, I'm surprised she's still alive. And that Njongo kid in Ward 16. Her mom is MIA and she's so weak she can't even keep her head up anymore. I could write you a whole list of names.

I should probably tear up this page. What would people think of me if they ever read this? It's the truth, though. Sometimes I wish some of them would die. It would be better for them and for me. I'm stretched so thin, Lord, if only there were fewer of them, then I could do more for the ones who have a chance.

❖

I can't be the worst doctor in history, surely? What about those doctors that lied about Steve Biko's death? What about that apartheid cardiologist who poisoned black people? I'm not like them. They are evil. I don't make mistakes on purpose. I'm just tired.

❖

Why don't I feel anything? Surely I should? All I feel is guilt for not caring, and fear of being caught out. They bore me, Lord, Your people bore me. I know it's wrong to say it, but they do. Their pain, their problems, their hopelessness, it all bores me. It's a constant reminder that the problems are vast, multiple, deep-rooted, and that there's nothing I can do to fix any of it. I don't deserve to call myself a Christian, because I don't behave like one. I lie to myself over and over again that I can do some good, but I can't. I can't change anything. It's all hopeless. They die no matter what I do.

❖

Someone once told me about this gas that's released from under the earth. Someone started a fire where it gathers, and it's never stopped burning to this day. It rages continuously, constantly, consuming everything around it, like the pits of hell.

That's how I feel inside. Like I've got a raging fire burning within me. It's too dangerous to go in there, and I don't know how to stop it from out here. It's a kind of hell inside. It's consuming me.

Maybe I'm just PMS-ing.

❖

I can't find peace. Not in my head, not in my heart, not in my soul, not anywhere.

❖

I used to like the Lord's Prayer. It's the only bit of the Bible I know off by heart, and as a child I would often say it over and over again when I began to feel scared. At times I would jumble up the words, say them upside down, but didn't think it mattered. I didn't think You would care, just as long as I kept saying the words. And it would work. It always worked. Sometimes it took longer than at other times, but it always made me feel better. Now nothing works.

❖

I so desperately want to be different, Lord. I want to walk into the wards and see the pools of tears and be moved by them. I don't want to be selfish and irritable and impatient. I don't want to be an obstacle in Your path. But this is how You made me.

❖

We were given last Friday off to go and vote in the municipal elections. Only the doctors on call had to go in. I couldn't convince my body to get out of bed. I wasn't sure if I was even registered to vote. I didn't know who I would vote for anyway, so I never left the house. On Monday morning Nyasha looked at me in disgust when I used my black anesthetic-drug marker to put a fake voting dot on my right thumb. She called me pathetic, and lectured me on how much had been lost for my right to vote. She told me how my ancestors would shower misfortune on my future because I didn't value my freedom. She said I was a disgrace.

I asked her how she thought her ancestors felt about her running away from her own country to come make a nuisance of herself here. She didn't respond, and I could see my words had hurt her. Well, so be it. If she can dish it out, she should be able to take it.

❖

I'm hungry, but food is the last thing I want to eat.

❖

There must be more than this.

Sir, give me this water so that I won't get thirsty and have to keep coming here to draw water.

John 4:15

Coke, KFC, Red Bull, those microwave meals that take up so much space in the fridge, vitamin water, coconut water, cayenne pepper water, holy water. Xanax, vodka, anything just to numb the feeling. Diet pills for energy. Ritalin to stay up at night. The morning-after pill. Mirena for those with more determination. Post-exposure prophylaxis at least four times a year. TB treatment for the unfortunate few. Flu vaccine. Hepatitis B booster. Third-generation cephalosporin at the sight of a sneeze. Scabies, a gift from the psychiatry ward. Eczema, asthma pumps, yoga, tofu, detox when on leave, fifteen days of eating green. Dubai or Thailand to make up for it all. Then you're back and the assault begins again.

❖

I had to leave the operating room this morning because I'd developed such severe menstrual cramps I could hardly keep myself from falling over and contaminating the entire operative field. It was odd. Although my periods had reduced to little more than spotting after the endometrial ablation, the monthly cramps had persisted like clockwork, maybe as a reminder that the beast is not dead, only sleeping. Doctor Sage said I should unscrub and go put my head down in the Anesthetics tea room until the next case arrives. While I was in there I texted Nyasha and asked if she could bring me ibuprofen from the emergency department. Sister Dlamini sat across the room, watching us as Nyasha took two tablets out of her pocket and offered me her bottled water. I could see she wanted to say something, but I couldn't have anticipated the words that came out of her mouth.

"Sies doctor!" she exclaimed. "*O na le sebete ne? Batho ba ga se batho*. You can get sick drinking from their bottles."

I couldn't believe she could say that right in front of Nyasha.

"She's just dumb," I mumbled to Nyasha as she picked up her stuff and prepared to head back to the emergency department.

Nyasha shrugged. "It's just a period South Africa's in," she said matter-of-factly. "Growing pains."

"Like period pain," I said, trying to make a joke. "Yeah." She gave me a weak smile. "Like period pain."

❖

I didn't tell Nyasha that I saw a cat coming out from under the table when we were out for dinner tonight, or that there were Portuguese men at the window. I can tell Nyasha most things, but this I'd never tell her. I know for sure she'd leave

me if she began to worry I might be going mad. I can't risk
that. She'd stay in the flat but pull away, watch me, analyze
my words. Some things you never say. You write them in
your journal but tell no one.

❖

Kgomotso's aunt approached me today. I've noticed her
in the ward, watching us as we go about our business,
but I've never heard her speak. Sometimes I've caught her
staring at me, but if my eyes meet hers, she turns away
shyly. So when she came up to me and asked whether I
thought Kgomotso was going to die, I was a little taken
aback. She pointed to Kgomotso's intravenous line that
was drawing blood, pointed to her own belly, which she
shared had a growing baby inside, and began to cry. I
mentioned You, told her the intravenous line was nothing
to worry about, that we would flush it as soon as we got
a chance, asked how far along she was. But she insisted.
Said she was alone in Johannesburg and without work,
and that there was no money to send a corpse to the East-
ern Cape.

I didn't know what to say, Lord, because Kgomotso *is*
going to die. You know it, I know it, and Kgomotso's aunt
knows it.

So I called Sister Lebea, who fetched a stool for all of us
to sit on. I hadn't thought to do that. They spoke without

too many words. Sister Lebea explained to Kgomotso's aunt that Kgomotso was likely to die on the road if she was put on a bus, but that there was a man with a van who was good and did this kind of thing. She spoke of a collection that the nurses took, a raffle, that wasn't much but would be enough, and that they would give her some of that. To Kgomotso, who had been sitting quietly in the bed listening to her fate being candidly discussed, Sister joked that she needed to take a bath, that she was becoming lazy wasting her days away in that hospital bed. Didn't she know a woman should be up before the sun? Kgomotso smiled a thin smile. I felt my eyes fill with water, but dared not release the tears. Instead I pressed my arm into Sister Lebea's as we sat together tightly on that stool, shoulder to shoulder, pretending it was all I could do to keep from falling off. We got up together. She told me to collect the Refusal of Hospital Treatment form and sign it. I did, and gave Kgomotso a pen. Sister was quick to chide me. "No pen, Doctor, get ink for a thumbprint." I did, and thanked her.

"Yes, Doctor," was her response as she pulled a teabag from her large cooler bag and sat down for a cup of tea.

Kgomotso died that very afternoon, before her aunt returned with the man with the van, before Sister had fetched the money from the collection, before I had had an opportunity to complete her discharge summary. She could have waited. Dying people are selfish. She should have waited.

❖

Nobody had bothered to tell me to my face that Tshiamo
was dead. Instead Ma came into my room while I was pretending to sleep and whispered it in my ear. When I con-
fronted her about this months later, she said Aunty Petunia
had advised her that this was the best way to break difficult
news to children, while their spirits were hovering over their
bodies.

I emailed Tshiamo about that, too. I put a lot of LOLs in
that email because I knew it would make him laugh. He'd
always thought Aunty Petunia was a stupid old woman just
waiting to steal the expensive plates Papa had left for Ma
when he moved out.

❖

Sometimes I can feel my lips curling into a snarl and my
eyebrows burying themselves deeply to form a line across
my forehead. When I catch myself doing this I quickly try
to correct it, try to convince the muscles in my face to
relax, the bones of my jaw to let go a little. I wonder how
I look as my face contorts into an ugly knot. The anxiety
in my heart is so full it brims over, seeping into my blood
and poisoning even the hair that grows out of my flesh.

❖

Ma called today. She asked if I was still living with "that Zimbabwean girl." She wants me to come home and go to the cemetery with her this weekend. I lied and said I'd be on call.

❖

Sometimes, in the very early hours of the morning when I'm driving home from a split-call and it's just me and the night lights on the empty highway, I let go of the steering wheel just for a second and push down hard on the accelerator, and wonder, if I were to go fast enough, would I take off into the sky and soar like a plane? Disappear into the darkness of the night? And if I were to land on the other side, would Tshiamo be there?

❖

This doesn't interest You, does it?

I know, I know, You're busy saving lives in Sudan. Never mind.

Part 2

The heart is deceitful above all things and desperately wicked: who can know it?

Jeremiah 17:9

Last night Mamokgheti Sesing of Vukani News told the world that a mob of twenty South African men set a street of shops belonging to a community of Somalians in Sechaba township alight. In addition, three young Somalian girls were stoned to death, and many families had to flee their homes. They showed a woman who'd been beaten by the crowd crying outside her ashen store, her children staring wide-eyed into the camera.

I called Nyasha immediately, but she didn't answer. It was perhaps a blessing, because I had no idea what I was going to say. When I went to the bathroom in the early hours of the morning, I heard her crying on the phone, telling her mother, far away in the UK, that she was afraid to open her mouth in public places in case people heard she was foreign and hurt her, too.

I was angry. How could we be so savage, so cruel, so inhumane? What kind of people are we?

I wanted to make things better. I set my alarm and resolved to tell Nyasha in the morning that those murderers didn't represent the ordinary South African.

They were criminals, mobsters, lowlifes. But as the thought entered my mind, I knew it was a lie. I thought of Ma, how she frowns every time I mention Nyasha and refuses to try the food she's cooked. Ma—church-going, God-fearing, people-loving Ma.

I remembered laughing myself in first-year varsity when Zanele called them all *oorkants* and refused to share a dorm room with one because she said they smelled of menstrual blood.

So when Nyasha walked into the kitchen this morning, eyes all puffed up, sclera bloodshot, I pretended not to notice. I acted like it was just another Thursday morning and played dumb.

Of course I'm ashamed. But it's not our fault. It's the white people's fault, Lord. Everything is. They taught us to hate ourselves. They made us like this. We weren't like this before they came. This is not the way we would have been if they hadn't come and messed everything up for everyone.

❖

Throughout the day the TV has been ablaze with burning shacks, burning shops, and burned people. The streets are crawling with bloodthirsty men calling for foreigners to leave the country. Nyasha came home a little after me and went straight to her room and hasn't stirred since. So I watched the news alone with the sound on mute. They showed images of a naked man being dragged by a mob of boys, blood gushing from his head, and then an image of a group of policemen pouring water over the body of an elderly woman. Hammers, axes, knives, bottles, sticks, rocks, men, women, children, animals everywhere.

Of course it was difficult to watch. But I had to. I had to face this horrible thing that we've become.

❖

Things have gotten worse. The xenophobic violence has spread like wildfire. On my call last night, the Emergency Medical Services brought in a foreign national who'd been burned alive and sustained third-degree burns to 80 percent of his body.

When Nyasha came home, the first thing she said was that she'd heard that a victim of the xenophobic violence was a patient of mine. She wanted to know what ward he was in so she could go and see him and give support to his family.

He wasn't my patient, I told her. He'd arrived already intubated on my emergency department call and I prescribed fluids, antibiotics, and analgesia, and then handed him over to the surgical team.

"Which ward is he in?" she'd insisted. "And what's his name?"

I explained that I last saw him in the emergency department on a ventilator, waiting for the surgeons to take over. They were aware of him but were held up in surgery. So I didn't know which ward he'd ended up in. Probably ICU or Burns Ward. I didn't remember his name.

"You just *left* him there?" she retorted accusatorily.

"I couldn't get an ICU bed, Nyasha," I tried to explain. "I called the surgery register and handed him over. But with third-degree burns to 80 percent of his body, you know *mos*, Nyasha, the treatment would probably only be supportive."

"So you did nothing?"

"I couldn't get a bed, Nyasha. What was I supposed to do?"

"Did you call Imhotep Academic Hospital?"

"Of course I called Imhotep," I lied. "You know it's always full."

"So you went back to bed?"

"Nyasha, for goodness sake, he had third-degree burns to 80 percent of his body, his chances of surviving were slim to none. I put up a line, we gave him good analgesia and antibiotics, and then handed him over to the surgical team. I'm a house officer, I'm not Jesus. What on earth was I supposed to do?"

"What is his name? Tell me his name so I can go back to the hospital and find him."

"I can't remember, Nyasha. It was a really busy call, the emergency department was packed. There were so many patients, I honestly can't remember."

"You don't even know his name?"

"Nyasha? Do you remember the names of every patient you see on call?"

"You don't care, do you? He's just another foreigner to you, another *kwere-kwere*!"

"Nyasha, come on, don't say that. You know that's not true."

"Where's the family? How did he get there? He couldn't have come alone."

"Emergency Medical Services brought him in, Nyasha, but I didn't ask where they found him. I'm sorry, I should have, but I didn't think to ask, with the third-degree burns to 80 percent of his body and all."

"You're pathetic. You're all the same. Fucking monsters."

"Nyasha! I'm sorry about what's happening with these xenophobic attacks, I really am, but it's not fair to take it out on me. I didn't do anything wrong."

"Didn't do anything wrong? You leave a helpless man, who's burned throughout his whole body by *your* people, to die in casualty with a drip in his arm and some Brufen, and you tell me you did nothing wrong? What kind of animal are you? Do you think those nurses and those surgery registrars who despise us foreigners are going to make an effort to attend to that man properly, sit on the phone and find him an ICU bed, give him a fighting chance? Why didn't you stay with him? Why didn't you stay on the phone? Why didn't you call Hamilton Naki Academic or Mary Malahlela Central Hospital? Why didn't you get the specialist on the line? What about a central venous pressure line? Did you catheterize him? How were you monitoring those fluids you were pouring into him? Did you consider any of that? You were the only chance he had, and instead you chose to go back to bed. You think you're different, Masechaba, but you're all the same."

The nurses had called him Maputo when they handed him over to me, and I hadn't gotten an opportunity to check his real name. A stab-chest had come in at the same time, and I needed a signature for putting in a chest drain for my Health Professionals Council of South Africa logbook, so I'd rushed across to assist with that patient. I hadn't forgotten about Maputo, and I knew that sorting him out would take much of the night, so I wanted to get the chest drain out of the way first. But by the time I got back to him, one of the medical students had already put up a line and tried to call Imhotep to see if there was an ICU bed, but reported that there wasn't one. So I prescribed antibiotics and analgesia and handed him over to the surgical team. And it wasn't Brufen. I wouldn't have given him Brufen, I'm not an idiot. Maybe I should have called Imhotep myself. Maybe I should have sat on the phone and tried Hamilton Naki, Mary Malahlela Central Hospital, the White House! Maybe I could have handled the case better. I didn't think of a central venous pressure line and I'm pretty sure he had a catheter in already or the nurses put it in, but I remember seeing one. I should have checked his name, though. I'm sure I did, because surely I wouldn't have written Maputo on his medical notes. Or maybe his real name was Maputo. Foreigners often change their names when they arrive in South Africa. Gosh, I don't know. Maybe I did mismanage him, but that wasn't because he was foreign, and I won't accept Nyasha's accusation that I treated him badly because he was foreign. That's bullshit. I take so much crap from the nursing staff and other doctors for being friends with her, from Ma for living with her. They call me a *kwere-kwere* lover behind my back, for goodness sake! So what she's saying is absolute crap and I won't accept it. Nyasha can go to hell.

❖

Things are spiraling out of control. One of the Nigerian doctors was spat on by a patient yesterday. According to the other interns, the patient said she didn't want to be examined by a cockroach. Many of the foreign doctors are now saying they don't feel safe coming to work. And Nyasha is still not speaking to me over the whole burn-patient thing.

It's crazy, Lord. This is crazy. What have we become?

I've resolved that I must do something to stop this. Or at least try.

I'm going to draw up a petition. I'll print it and distribute it around the morning departmental meetings. I'll get all the other interns to sign it, too, deliver it to the doctors' quarters, put it under everybody's doors. I'll stick it up at the blood bank and in the lab so that students coming to fetch results can sign it while they wait. Maybe even at the security gate. As people sign themselves in they could simultaneously sign the petition, too. I could even walk around the cafeteria at lunchtimes, table to table, and ask people to sign. I could leave it in the anesthetists' tea room so they could sign it between cases. Maybe even in the Emergency Department, as people wait, I could ask families of patients to sign it, too. And if the CEO of the hospital signs it, and the senior leadership, maybe I could even write to the local newspaper. Maybe it could make it to the Minister of Health and the minister could sign it. Maybe I could even get in touch with other interns on the intern Facebook page and ask them to circulate it to other hospitals. Maybe eventually it could become a countrywide thing for the whole nation to sign. Then the world will see that this isn't who we are, and that those thugs out there going around killing foreigners don't represent the majority of us. Maybe this petition will bring this madness to an end.

But I won't tell Nyasha. I want to do this all by myself. I want to surprise her. Then she will see just how much I love her, just how different I am, just how much I care.

❖

Oh my gosh, Lord, I myself cannot believe how many people have signed the petition. It's had 3,000 Shares on

Facebook and 10,000 Likes. I had a call this morning from a lady from SAFM who wants to interview me about what we're doing. I also got a mention in the *Mail & Guardian Online* and the journalist at the end of the article challenged doctors around the country to do the same and stand up to xenophobia.

Lord, it's so strange, You know. I always knew You were going to use me for something important, but I couldn't have guessed it would be this. It really feels great to be at the forefront of something good. I can't remember the last time I achieved something single-handedly. I'm finally coming into my own. The *Mail & Guardian* described me as a young activist, an inspiration. I've never thought of myself as an activist, as inspiring to anyone, but there it all was, and they said it, not me.

I made the mistake of telling Sister Palesa about the article and the potential radio interview, and that the success of the petition had gotten me thinking about organizing an anti-xenophobia march in the community. Instead of congratulating me on the success of the initiative, she showered me with criticism. I was going to land myself in trouble, she said. This wasn't the suburbs. People here are really suffering, she said, and foreigners are largely to blame.

"People can't feed their families, Doctor. These foreigners are eating everything. If it's not the Nigerians, it's the Somalis. If it's not the Somalis, it's the Chinese. Enough with this petition nonsense now, or you're really going to irritate people and get yourself hurt. Focus on your work. People around here don't like it when children don't know how to behave."

When I got home this afternoon I told Nyasha what Sister Palesa had said. Nyasha said she wasn't surprised. Perhaps it was better to stop. She didn't want me getting hurt.

"These people are crazy, Masechaba. And anyway, going on radio and everything is an unnecessary amount of attention. These things are delicate political matters. Leave it to the real activists."

I'm annoyed. Here I am trying to do a good thing, trying to stand up for something I believe in. And the people around me who should be supporting me, who should be proud of me, are telling me to stop because the community will be irritated? Really? Who gives a fuck about the community? What's happening is wrong, and if *we* don't stand against what's wrong, who will? You'd think Nyasha of all people would get this. I finally have a cause, something to wake up for, something to hang myself on, and Nyasha wants to take that away from me? No, I'm going to see this thing through. Was it not Nyasha who chastised me for allegedly neglecting that burn patient from Mozambique? Was she not the same person who swore at me for not doing more? And now that I *am* doing more, she has nothing but discouragement for me. The same Nyasha who goes running around to poetry sessions, criticizing African presidents whose countries she knows nothing about, insisting that we must put an end to white supremacy once and for all, tells me to leave this noble cause to "the real activists"? I *am* an activist! The *Mail & Guardian* said so. She's probably just jealous. Forget Nyasha. What I'm doing is bigger than her, and she'll thank me in time.

Part 3

I say to myself, I will not mention His name, I will speak in His name no more. But then, it becomes like a fire burning in my heart, imprisoned in my bones. I grow weary holding it in, I cannot endure it.

Jeremiah 20:9

Why are You still here?

❖

Go away!

❖

Where were You when it happened? Did You watch? Did You cringe? Did You cry? Did You know all day? As I washed my face and brushed my teeth, chose my under-wear and pulled on my scrub pants, did You know already that they'd later be ripped, that my tongue would be torn and my front teeth cracked?

Did You pity me, God?

How long have You known for? From the day before yes-terday or the day before that? From my seventh birthday or the day of my birth? And all this time as I giggled and laughed and blew out candles on cakes, You knew this lay on my horizon and You said and did nothing?

And if You cared, because You claim You do, did You watch? All of it? From beginning to end? With eyes wide open? Was there no knot for me in Your stomach, no lump in Your throat? Me, Your child? You watched them rape me and didn't blink, didn't even blink. You, God, watched them tear me apart, divide me among themselves, and You stood and stared.

Or did You run and hide? See none of it at all? Only hear about it later?

Or were You out of town, away on business, saving lives somewhere else?

So now You come and You want to help me? Now, after the event, You want to console me? That's very nice. That's very, very nice.

Go away!

❖

Why do You want to see us grovel? Why must we break first into millions of pieces before You shovel us off the floor? Why must we shatter first before You react? Why must we pray for things that are obvious? Wasn't it obvious that I needed You to save me?

Go away!

❖

Nyasha would mock me if she knew I still wrote to You.

❖

I can't sleep.

❖

Our Father in heaven . . .
How could You let it happen?

❖

Stay calm, breathe slow, think less.

❖

Lord, please give me a hug. If You're there, please give me
a hug.

❖

I'm so scared.

❖

Do You hate me?

❖

Who are You, anyway, and why should I care what You think? Where do You come from? How can I trust You when You have no home, no people who call You their own?

Just leave me alone.

❖

Please Jesus, come now. Please don't leave me.

❖

I wish this was all just a really long, really bad dream.

❖

I took a bath today. Ma cried. I cried. Ma said, "Everything will be fine." I told her not to lie. Ma cried some more.

❖

I wish I could disappear.

❖

You'd think You, being the ruler of the universe, could take a large damp cloth, spray it with bleach and wipe all of this away. Or press a reset button, or pull out the batteries, disconnect the cord, or something, anything. Put me in a deep sleep and make it all a dream.

But You won't, will You?

❖

I don't even know why I speak to You. You never speak back. Your silence is everywhere. It's thick and plugs out the air. It's outside and inside, making it hard to breathe, hard to believe.

❖

I prayed daily. I prayed DAILY. I PRAYED DAILY. I PRAY DAILY. I PRAY DAILY! Are You deaf? Why do You not hear me? Why can't You see me? Here I am. Strike me down, please! I want to die.

❖

Lord, I'm sorry. Will You get under the covers with me, please? If I ask You nicely, will You do it, please? If You're there, please don't leave me here alone.

❖

Is it because I didn't wear my rosary to work? Are You mad at me? Is it because I didn't vote? Or is this about François?

I only let him finger me, Lord. That's all we did. Surely You can't be so cruel?

Or is this supposed to be the "thorn in my flesh"? This is no thorn, Lord, this is a dagger!

What did I do to deserve this?

❖

Okay, never mind. Just go. Go be wherever else You need to be. Leave me be.

❖

Sister Agnes came to visit me today. She brought scones with her and a recycled card that said "Happy Birthday" on the front. It had a kitten on it with big cartoon-like eyes. Inside she had scratched out the "Happy Birthday" and written "Condolences." She told me some of the interns had written a letter of complaint to the National Department of Health. They passed it around from one departmental morning meeting to the next, asking for signatures to support the letter stating that security on the hospital premises needs to be improved. She said the superintendent had ordered pepper spray and whistles for everyone to wear at night. She said they were praying for me every day. She said I should pray, too, that God would help me.

Help me with what, I wondered. What could this God possibly do for me now?

❖

The visitors pour through the door. I feel like an animal in a zoo. Ma says they only want to show me their support; it's better not to be alone for too long. But they irritate me, saying stupid things like, "Everything will be okay, don't worry, everything will be okay." How do they know everything will be okay? Why do they say stupid things they have no evidence for?

Things that are impossible to guarantee. "Everything will be okay." They say it with such confidence. Liars! Where is their evidence? Everything will be okay? No, it won't. Nothing is okay. Absolutely nothing.

If people don't know what to say they shouldn't say anything at all.

❖

Maybe I didn't pray right. Maybe I didn't pray long enough, soft enough, hard enough . . . maybe I said the wrong prayer, too many prayers, vague prayers . . . maybe my prayers were insincere, unconvincing, repetitive, boring . . .

Give me a second chance, please. Teach me how to pray the way You want and I'll do it. I'll do it every day, twice a day, all day. Please, just make this all a bad dream. Take all of this away, please, Lord. Please.

❖

What is the point of us being here on earth if everything's all about heaven? If You don't want to/don't care to/can't change anything here on earth, what's the point really? If it's all completely random and just about struggling through to the end that will eventually come, why do we bother?

If this is temporary, why can't I just fast-forward to the inevitable and kill myself?

In fact, I will kill myself. You think I'm scared to? I'm not. I'm just too weak right now, but once my energy comes back, I'll do it, I'll kill myself. Just You wait and see.

❖

Will You really send me to hell if I kill myself? Even though I love You so much? Even though I'd be doing it to get closer to You?

❖

Being alive is the most dangerous thing in the world. Anything can happen at any time. It's safer to be dead.

❖

This wasn't the way things were supposed to be for me. This was not the plan.

❖

I'm so sick of hearing about Job. Everybody wants to tell me about Job. The story of Job isn't comforting. I don't care if it has a happy ending. It doesn't make me feel any better to know that he had everything replaced in the end. Some things just can't be replaced.

❖

Ma asked if the voices are gone. What voices? What voices? She looks at me like she's scared of me. I see her watching me as she hurries up and down the passage.

What voices, Lord?

She brings me the daily newspaper, then fruit, then rusks, then chips, then tea, then porridge, then bread, then peanuts. I can't eat all this food, and the newspapers make me sad.

What voices?

❖

I'm bleeding again.

❖

Fix me.
   Fix me.
   Fix me.
   Heal me.
   Heal me.
   Heal me.
   Are You not the Great Physician? Or should we wait for somebody else?

❖

It's been a while since I bled like this, since drops of serum and cells of hemoglobin have dripped past my thighs, day after day, so that all that's left coming out is water. It's been years since I've felt such rage for the dysfunctional flesh within my pelvis, years since I've wanted to stick my fist all the way up my vagina and yank the demon out.

❖

Will it always be like this?

❖

I pee slowly. Not fast like before, when I was somebody with things to do and people waiting for me. I pee slowly so it doesn't burn. I pee slowly because my mind is idle and there's nowhere else it needs to be.

❖

Sometimes when I'm forgetting, drifting into mindlessness, I'm jolted by a breath on the back of my neck, a breath like the one that breathed on me before grabbing me from behind and bringing my legs to the floor. I begin to cry out. Ma says it's just a breeze, that the doors and burglar bars and gates are all locked, and nobody can hurt me in here. But that breath gets in somehow, under the door, through the burglar bars, over the gate. I feel it warm and moist on my neck. I tell Ma she must stop bringing me all these newspapers and use them to plug the windows, the doors, the holes in the walls. But she gets angry when I say these things. She says she won't allow me to surrender my mind to madness.

❖

If I feel myself beginning to get anxious, if the thoughts in my head begin to move at an ever-increasing pace and there seem to be others threatening to start a conversation in my mind, I cover my head with my pillow and force sleep. Sleep works better than all the anxiolytics Dr. Phakama prescribed, because when I wake up I've forgotten and for minutes, sometimes even up to an hour, I exist lightly, like a being without a care in the world.

❖

Ma says that Philippians 4 says I mustn't be anxious, but through prayer and petition, with thanksgiving, I should present my requests to God.

I'm not sure what kind of petition You mean, Lord, but I henceforth pray with a thankful heart that You take my life.

Amen.

❖

Can You hear me? Do You even care?

Did You not say, "Seek and ye shall find, knock and the door shall be opened"? Didn't You say that? Can't You hear me knocking? Can't You see me seeking? Hello! I want to die!

❖

I don't know why I bother.

❖

03:02 . . . 03:02 . . . 03:02

What is it about this time of night that drags me from sleep, pulls my eyelids open, shakes my mind awake? There were three men and they divided me in two? Or was it three times two?

03:02 . . . 03:02 . . . 03:02 . . . time after time.

Do they sleep, Lord? Do they dream of parties and balloons and picnics with smiling faces? Or are they tormented, like me? Do they have to fight off whispers, images, shadows that hide in the recesses of their minds?

❖

It's probably not healthy to be up this late.

❖

Time moves slowly. Tshiamo's old watch calls from my dressing table drawer.

"*Chronos, kairos, chronos, kairos . . .*"

I wore it until the strap withered, and then carried it in my pocket until the face fell and cracked. So now it sits in my drawer raising its voice from time to time.

❖

They said at Sunday school that You're outside of time, so I'd pray sometimes on those calls at the hospital, when my feet were swollen, my eyes red and dry, my hands scratchy from repeated washes with alcohol-based soap, that You'd stretch the thirty minutes I had to rest my head before the ward round to thirty days. That, if it was at all possible, You'd grant me the small indulgence of stretching time for just a moment so I could recover.

When I told Nyasha about this prayer she said it was (a) stupid and (b) selfish.

"What about some woman somewhere out there who's being raped? Would she thank you for turning her thirty minutes of horror into thirty days?"

I remembered that conversation as I lay motionless on that cold floor, and hoped no foolish intern out there was praying that time would stop for them.

❖

I know in my head that this would be the time to turn to Jesus and ask for peace. Maybe I could find some solace and comfort there. But I've never had any sense of direction, and I don't know which way that is and how to get there.

❖

I've decided to stop all the medication. I'm tired. I've actually come to like it, this little trickle of blood coming out of me day after day. It colors the bathwater a pretty pink. Sometimes when a tiny clot comes out, the water goes dark maroon.

The soft part of my belly is warm and tingly. I'm so faint, I have to sit often, to keep from falling over. It's a kind of pain, a kind of pleasure, a kind of freedom that I like, that Dr. Phakama's medication tried to steal from me. But it's mine and it's nice and I want it.

And the background whispers, they're okay, too. They keep me company, sing me songs and tell me stories that help to pass the time. Your silence was anyway far too loud.

❖

I think I see a cockroach, but when I turn my head it's a scratch in the wall, a candy wrapper on the floor, a chip in the tiles.

❖

In the mornings I sit on the edge of my bed. I imagine it's a tall building, or a bridge, a cliff, a roof, the balcony of a skyscraper. I fantasize about what it would be like to fly off and come crashing to the floor.

How does a mind unravel? Axon by axon? Fiber by fiber? And when it's psychotic, where are You? Are You far from me or are You near?

Do You remember that psychiatric patient in Ward 12 who used to sing on the edge of his bed in the early hours of the morning? He'd sing old hymns, beckoning the day in, as his mind lay in the pills hidden under his pillow. He had a beautiful voice and I often had to step into the doctors' office just to collect myself before I could do my rounds. On those mornings it didn't seem so bad to be mad. It seemed the madness was a welcome freedom from the badness of our world. On those mornings I was less afraid of the cracks I'd begun to sense in my own psyche. On those mornings I allowed myself to relax a little about the vulnerability of my mental health.

He didn't stay very long. His urinary tract infection responded well to antibiotics and he was sent back to Sweet Rivers. The next morning there was another man in his bed, an angry smoker whose larynx had been cut out to stop the cancer creeping out of his lungs and into the rest of his body. A moody, bitter man who seemed bent on coughing up the yellow phlegm from his infected surgical wound in the direction of any staff member who dared approach.

❖

I had a bad dream. Nyasha was here, in this room, her hands were on my throat.

She was angry, shouting. "You Saffas, look how fat you've become, look how thick your necks are now. You've become too comfortable. You think the food will never run out. You eat so much you don't even realize that someday it will finish and you'll be left eating each other!"

Then the men came and they were laughing, taunting me.

"You like your *kwere-kwere pipi*, ne? That's because you've never had a real South African man. Today we will make you a real South African woman."

And then there was blood pouring out of me, between my things, gushing, spraying, splashing everywhere. It covered their legs, then their arms, then their heads, drowning them, drowning me.

❖

How does one move one's mind past the thoughts that threaten to destroy everything? There are stains on my legs and they won't come off. When I bathe I try to scrub them, but they won't come off. I showed Ma and told her that nothing will ever be the same again.

She said she couldn't see anything, that there's nothing on my legs, nothing anywhere. That I look just the same.

She said she knows I haven't been taking my pills. Said I've come so far already, and begged me not to give in.

"Give in to what, Ma?"

"To the madness, Masechaba."

"What madness, Ma?"

"The madness, Masechaba, the madness that has done all these things to you. The madness that has stolen my child. The madness that has stolen your life. The madness that makes you sit on a bucket, wiping yourself with news- papers, covering the floor and the walls with blood. The madness that is killing you, Masechaba. The madness that will kill me."

She cried so much, Lord. I felt so bad, so bad that I'd brought her—all of us—so much pain.

"I'm sorry, Ma."

❖

Am I sick, Lord? Is my mind sick?

❖

How did this happen? How did You let this happen?

❖

Is it because I didn't vote? Was Nyasha right?

❖

Sometimes they shout.

"Why must you talk so loud?" I ask them. "Why must you be so noisy? Whisper! I can hear you. Whisper."

But they don't listen, and it makes me confused. Are they outside or inside? So I put in my wax earplugs to try to muffle them out.

❖

Ma thinks if we perhaps go to the cemetery and speak to Koko and Malome and Mamogolo and Rangwane and Rakgadi and Ntate and Abuti and Gogo and Ousi and Mani that maybe they can help me. That maybe from where they are in heaven they can intercede, negotiate, speak to You, plead with You on my behalf. She says she doesn't know how to help me, but that they will.

She says maybe these things happened because I didn't tell the ancestors I had graduated. I didn't tell them I was now working, didn't tell them where I worked and that it wasn't safe, that I'd be doing twenty-four-hour calls, so I'd have to work at night. Ma thinks it's all down to a miscommunication between me and the ancestral realm, and if I'd only spoken, all this could have been avoided.

It makes me angry. Are they dumb, these ancestors of mine? Are they stupid, dense, dull? Don't they see from their heavenly heights what happens here? Why must they be told about everything, forewarned, given beat-by-beat updates? Why must the obvious be explained to these gods?

Ma says I shouldn't speak like this. She says my problem is that I've always been disdainful and listened to no one, that my rash mouth will bring me bad luck.

I laughed when she said that.

What kind of luck does she think I have?

❖

I'm sorry.

Maybe this is all my own doing. I should have voted. I shouldn't have let that white boy play with my vagina. I should never have started that petition. I should have gone to the cemetery. I shouldn't have stopped my medication. I shouldn't have written all this blasphemous crap in this journal. I should have been less excited. In life one should never be too excited. That's when bad things happen. I was too happy, running around with that petition. I wasn't focused. Instead I was daydreaming about François, who didn't even know how to pronounce my name properly.

Sister Agnes had warned me. "Doctor, why do you wear such nice clothes to a call? We don't dress like that for overnight calls."

Sister Palesa had warned me. "Doctor, the community is not happy with this petition thing. You're getting too carried away."

But I wouldn't listen. I needed to look nice at work because people had started to recognize me from the anti-xenophobia press coverage. I should have listened. I should have been calmer, quieter, more thoughtful, more focused. I was too, too excited. That's why those men raped me.

❖

I see their faces from time to time. The one with the striped T-shirt, his belly protruding beneath it. I instinctively force my eyes shut, hope the tears will wash the images out of my mind.

Be still and know that I am God.
Be still and know that I am God.
Be still and know that I am God.

I whisper the words into the night. They fall from my lips, but escape my heart.

❖

There is no vocabulary for the pain I feel. How do I construct a sentence that explains that they made me into a shell of myself? Not "like" a shell of myself, but an actual shell of myself? How do I explain that what they stole from me is more than just my "womanhood" or any of that condescending stuff people like to talk about, but a thing that once lost can never be found because it is unnamed? How do I explain that the languages at my disposal can't communicate the turmoil I have inside? That it's more than my "dignity" they stole, it's more than a "violation" they subjected me to? That it would have been better to die than to be spooned out and left that way?

❖

We saw Dr. Phakama again today. I saw her writing in her notes that I'm "preoccupied with internal stimuli." She thought I couldn't see, forgetting that I, too, am medically trained. She explained that severe depression can result in psychosis, that it is important I stay on the medication.

I wanted to tell her she was wrong, that my mind began to come apart a long time ago, long before any of this happened, long before François encouraged me to try the smelly cheese at the Christmas party, long before I pretended to enjoy the rot so he could think I was sophisticated. Long before I began to pay in blood.

But she wouldn't let me get a word in.

She told me about the importance of getting out of bed, of picking up the things I used to enjoy, of reclaiming my old life.

"Your mother says you used to write beautiful poems. How about you pick that up again? Maybe you can write about what has happened, write about this difficult time. Maybe that will be of help to you. You might just find this difficult time is a blessing in disguise."

A blessing in disguise? What an extravagantly sophisticated disguise! What a spectacularly deceptive disguise!

Ma says we need to give Dr. Phakama a chance; that it was only the second session and that these counseling things take time. She says Dr. Phakama wasn't trying to be dismissive, just trying to be nice. I mustn't get so angry, or be so quick to write people off. I need to want to get better. People want to help me, but I need to want to be helped.

❖

Ma is right.

A good Christian wouldn't mourn this loss the way I am doing. It's only flesh, after all. It was only a penis, a couple of penises, entering a cavity that man decided to call a vagina. It's only muscles, blood vessels, nerves, mucus. It doesn't think, it doesn't remember, it doesn't even really feel, not in any enlightened way. It just responds to thrusts and vibrations. My heart still beats, air still fills my lungs, my limbs move fine. So why do I feel so hollow? Why does my blood run cold? Why does acid rise into my throat while my bowels fall to the floor?

❖

When the bishop came to visit our church, he preached that
we shouldn't hold on to anything too tightly, not our suc-
cesses, our health, our beauty, our intelligence, not even the
people we love. Not a thing, only God. I thought the bishop
a crazy man. Not even the people we love?

When Papa used to live with us, he would often say, "Why
do you talk so much? You're overconfident for a young lady.
Be humble, be quiet, rest a little."

When I was on call, telling patients why xenophobia was
wrong, Sister Agnes would say, "*Mara*, Doctor, *wena le dilo
tše tša gago, tlogela man! O tlo ipakela mathata.*"

But I didn't listen. I never listened to anyone, not even the
bishop. Always too full of excitement. I held on too tightly.
If I'd only just relaxed and let them penetrate, maybe they
wouldn't have hit me, maybe it wouldn't have taken so long.

❖

Father Joshua came to visit again today. He put oil on my
forehead and sprinkled holy water in my bedroom. I told
him what had happened, everything, from beginning to
end, sparing him nothing. I wanted him to hear every gory
detail, to see if his faith could stomach it. He prayed for me,
prayed for the men who raped me, asked that You forgive
them, "for they do not know what they do."

I didn't say "amen" at the end of that prayer. I don't
want You to forgive them. They knew exactly what they

were doing. If I die and land up in heaven, I don't want to have to see them there, I don't want to have to mingle with them. That's not the kind of heaven I want to be in.

❖

Maybe if they'd been drunk, I'd feel a little better about it all. But they weren't. There wasn't a drop of alcohol on their tongues. I know because those tongues were in my mouth, their saliva down my throat. They were sober, their minds clear as day. They knew exactly what they were doing, and they did it with such passion. They hated me so much. It was in their eyes, in their breath. I felt it on their skin. They were angry with me. They said I was a disappointment, that instead of helping my own people, I was running around with *kwere-kweres*, the very *kwere-kweres* that were ruining our country, stealing our jobs, using up our grants. Their children were starving because of these people and I was making that worse. Spoiled, foolish children like me needed to be taught a lesson, so others would see that the community didn't hesitate to discipline traitors. They said I was lucky they didn't necklace me, like they did to the likes of me during apartheid.

I wish they had. I wish they had just killed me.

❖

I remember walking into the Emergency Department after-
ward, and whispering, "Sister."

None of them responded. Not one of them lifted their
heads to notice that my shirt was torn, my mouth split, my
eyes blackened, and my pants soiled and bloodied. I tried
again. "Sister."

But without looking up, Sister Palesa simply pointed at
my box and said it was full of patients and that I needed to
work faster.

I couldn't remember the words to the hymns, the
ones that used to lift my spirits as Nyasha and I drove to
work, that got me through the long night calls and helped
me when God felt far and distant. The hymns Nyasha said
were lame, that made her embarrassed to be associated with
me. The ones Ma called white people's music.

I tried to sing them as I walked to the toilets to wash my
face, as I used wet toilet paper to wipe the dirt off my pants,
as I took the pile of patient files out of my box, as blood
trickled down the side of my leg. I tried to force the words
out of my mouth, but all that escaped was a silent cry.

"Oh Lord my God, when I in awesome wonder . . . Oh
Lord my God, when I in awesome wonder . . . Oh Lord my
God, when I in awesome wonder . . . Oh Lord my God . . ."

I wanted to sing God's praises, shout them, despite the
circumstances, but my tongue refused.

"Oh Lord my God . . . Oh Lord my God . . . Oh Lord
my God . . ."

When I recounted all of this to Dr. Phakama, she said I
must have been in the first stage of bereavement. After rape
one suffers a loss of the former self, she said, and it's normal
and important to mourn. She explained that there are five
stages of bereavement: denial, anger, bargaining, depression, and acceptance, and that my desire to sing praise to
my God after I'd just been raped was a textbook example
of extreme denial.

Denial. Denial. Denial.

A strange word. The refusal to admit the truth. Whose
truth?

❖

It didn't matter how clever, how careful, how disciplined I
was. I was disciplined! So I had a drink on occasion, so I got
really drunk at the Christmas party, but that's all. I've never
smoked a joint in my life, never done any drugs, never had
sex with François when I could have, when I wanted to. I got
into medical school. I studied all the time. I worked hard. I
prayed. Heaven knows I prayed. I exercised, used hand sani-
tizer, even kept antiseptic wet wipes in my bag. I was careful, I did everything right. But my floor collapsed and I fell,
then the sky fell in, then the whole universe fell in, crushing
me, the sky, the floor . . . and I still don't even know why.

❖

I think of the nurse in *The English Patient*. Perhaps if I'd cared for my patients the way she cared for hers? But she also slipped into his bed. So is it possible to love them and leave them there? Is it possible to love them without them leaving stains on one's heart? Does a heart have room for all of their pain (and one's own), for their broken bones (and one's shattered soul), for their discomfort (and one's own shame)?

❖

I'm haunted by the faces of the patients I neglected, rushed through, walked past, ignored. Those faces remind me every day that I only got what I deserved.

❖

The sessions with Dr. Phakama are a waste of time. She wants me to do relaxation exercises. She makes me sit with my eyes closed while she reads from a printed sheet that tells me to picture myself walking alone in a park.

"Find a quiet space where there are no people," she reads, "where you can be alone, where no one can see you and you can see no others. Find a tree, a tall towering tree, sit down, close your eyes, and rest your head against it."

Is she crazy? What is relaxing about the idea of being alone in a big, empty park behind some tree?

When I said this to her, she said I should use my imagination.

Heaven only knows where she downloaded this one from. Or perhaps she got it from a visiting lecturer as a student and has used it unimaginatively ever since. Where in the world is this technique helpful? Maybe somewhere in Europe women go alone to big, empty parks and sit behind trees with closed eyes to relax.

❖

I wish I could look inside and see if anything's broken. If my memory serves me right, the vagina is lined with squamous mucosa like the inside of the mouth, so it should have healed up pretty fast. But maybe it hasn't. Maybe it's severely damaged, rotting, like those necrotic cervixes after botched abortions.

❖

"I was raped."

Dr. Phakama wants me to say it. She says it will help. She says by putting it in the past tense I can overcome it.

But when it's your own life and you're living it, there is never so clear a distinction. I'm still being raped even now, even when I'm not. I can't say when one stopped and the other began. I am being rape.

❖

How viscous our blood must be. It carries so much in it. Stories swirling round and round our veins, up into our hearts at least a zillion times a day. Stories of men going into cities, men in men, men in women, women in men, children in women, men in children. Strangers living in each other's arteries, sharing intimacies, sharing pain, sharing anger, sharing hatred, sharing resentment, sharing loss.

Who are these terrorists that have invaded my blood, taken over my body?

❖

Ma came home triumphant this afternoon. She went to the flat to make sure the electricity was off, and it looked like Nyasha had moved out.

"At least one good thing has come out of this mess. Finally that Zimbabwean girl is out of your life."

When I asked Ma why Nyasha hadn't come to see me, she said Nyasha was probably still angry that I stabbed her for burning the mincemeat, but that who knows what is what with these foreigners? When I asked what she meant, what mincemeat, she said I shouldn't worry, I should just rest and "forget that girl."

I stabbed her? Did I stab Nyasha, Lord?

❖

"Major depression with psychotic features. It happens, Masechaba, particularly with your family history. You were especially vulnerable. You are unwell, but you'll get better. Nobody can blame you for the things a sick mind does, and you shouldn't blame yourself. I'm sure your friend understands, and from what your mother tells me, it wasn't really a stab, more like a small cut, and it wasn't very deep. These things happen to the best of us. Stay on your medication and you'll get better."

Dr. Phakama thinks she's some kind of prophet. What does she know about my family history? How dare she use Tshiamo against me? This has nothing to do with him. I'm nothing like Tshiamo.

She then had the nerve to say that there's a blog for women like me, for women who've been gang-raped.

"Correctively raped" as she called it, a rape to correct what their society deems abhorrent behavior. She says in our society many people don't like foreigners, and the men who raped me might have seen my behavior as threatening societal norms, and felt it their duty to correct me. She said this has been seen in the gay and lesbian community, but she hadn't seen it reported in the context of xenophobic violence. She said it would help to try to understand where the men were coming from. It would help my healing. She'd been thinking she and I might write a scientific paper about it together, if I was up to it. Of course she would be the first author, as it was her idea. But I would be acknowledged.

I wanted to tell her to go fuck herself. But I said nothing. I just resolved never to set foot in her offices again.

❖

How do they expect you not to lose your mind? They pull you open again and again, ram themselves into you again and again. Leave you with disease, warts, worms, pimples, pain, blood, rot coming out of your body. Your body! Why? Because of the gold mines, they tell you, because of the Dutch, because someone at some point stole from them, because they never had fathers, because of Zimbabwe and Shaka and the government, because of xenophobia, unemployment, apartheid, colonialism, because of history, because of the serpent, because of Adam and Eve. Because of anything and everything. Because they can.

Just because.

This is the problem of knowing, of knowing but not knowing, of knowing too much but not enough to fully understand. Webs and webs of lies. History is a con man; history writers change stories to suit the times (their times!) and memory is weak and unreliable. And truth? Any man's guess. And what of woman? The first fool.

❖

I called Tshiamo's phone today, to tell him what Dr. Phakama had said. That we're a family of mad people, him, me, Papa, Ma, all of us. That I was correctively raped. That I should sit in a park behind a tree with my eyes closed to help me get better.

"Hello, this is Tshiamo Lebea. I can't take your call right now. Please leave a message and I'll get back to you as soon as possible."

Tshiamo has always been a liar. After almost two years, I don't know why MTN hasn't disabled his voicemail.

"As soon as possible." How many times has he said that to me? "As soon as possible." I've left message after message on his phone and "as soon as possible" has never come. It will never come.

❖

Ma called Dr. Phakama and told her she caught me try-ing to call "my dead brother's phone." She's upset that I don't want to see Dr. Phakama anymore, and said that if I continue being difficult she'll have me forcibly admitted to Sweet Rivers. When I said nothing, she started crying. She said she won't lose another child to insanity. That the problem with me is I think I know everything and refuse to listen to anyone.

What do you say to that, really? If you try to defend your-self you only prove the very point she is trying to make.

Maybe she's right. Maybe I do think I know everything.

It's the explaining that gets to me. Dr. Phakama always wants an explanation; everything I say needs to be explained. Why this? Why that? Why must I always have to explain? Why can't people appreciate that some things can't be explained? Like why bells have been ringing all week, not even at the same time, not even for the same length of time, just ringing, from churches far out somewhere, or maybe from within my mind. Why does vinegar have such a strong smell but only a subtle taste, so that even when I pour on more and more so my fish and chips float on my plate I have to drink it with a teaspoon to taste it?

I'm not mad. I'm just tired.

❖

According to Dr. Phakama, my genes have been running from mental illness my whole life. Maybe it's finally caught up with me.

❖

Poor Ma: first Tshiamo, now me. Tshiamo was an idiot. He didn't have a good enough reason. What was he so tormented about, anyway? Why couldn't he just suck it up and make it work like the rest of us? Maybe if he'd been here none of this would have happened.

❖

I'm glad Tshiamo is dead. This rape thing would have killed him. His heart was always too small. It only had space for his own problems, nobody else's. And besides, I wouldn't want Tshiamo feeling sorry for me. I don't want anyone feeling sorry for me.

❖

Lord, there's so much pain in my heart. If only You would hold it for me, even for just a little while, so my weary soul might rest and my tired body recover.

❖

Is it because I worked on Sundays and didn't keep the Sabbath holy? Broke one of Your ten commandments? I had no choice. The call roster was drawn, the calls had to be done. Who was I not to work on a Sunday when everyone else does? Jesus's disciples picked wheat on the Sabbath, and He defended them. Why didn't He defend me? Is it because I'm not good enough? You say You love us all the same, but You don't, You love others differently. You love others more. Why didn't You defend me, Jesus?

❖

I looked in the mirror this morning. I stood before it with my towel at my feet to see what has been done to me. My body looks the same. I still have that weird malformed nail on my left baby toe, like a crumbly stone you can't put nail polish on. My eyes look the same. I think there might be bags under them, but those might have been there before. I have no scabs, no bruises. The stains I used to see seem to have disappeared. A bit of cramping, but maybe it's premenstrual pain. Otherwise I look exactly the same. If I didn't tell, no one would know.

❖

At least if I had become some sort of hero, some sort of martyr, at least if I was on the news and interviewed, at least if I wrote a book and people cried when they read it, at least if the United Nations had made me an ambassador or the Nobel Committee gave me a prize . . . But there's been nothing like that. The world did not notice. It just kept on spinning. People kept on getting into their cars in the morning and going to work. People kept on shopping, eating, laughing, loving, playing, and drinking wine. While my flesh was being split into two, then four, then eight, people were getting married, getting promoted, winning awards.

❖

Ma came back from church with fresh ideas. She said we mustn't underestimate evil. The devil doesn't sleep. He's just as active today as he was during apartheid. She says he's just learned to disguise himself better. He puts on masks so we can't identify him as easily as we used to. Even people who come across as friends may be using the devil's charms to take away what God has gifted us. So we mustn't underestimate how our success can make others jealous. Even people who we think love us, even friends, even our very closest friends. They can trick us, put curses on our lives and steal our joy.

"Ma," I say, because I know where this is going. "Nyasha has nothing to do with what happened."

"I'm just saying, Masechaba, be careful in the future with these foreigners. I know you have a big heart and you feel sorry for them, but they're not people like us. You think you know them, but how can you ever really know them unless you live in their countries and see how they do their things? We fought for the things we have. Three hundred years, Masechaba, we fought those colonizers. And as if that wasn't enough, we had to spend another fifty years fighting Afrikaners. And now these people want to come and steal the fruits of our struggle? Do you think that girl liked seeing how easy things were for you? She has to write extra exams and spend more years working in the government sector while you progress. Of course that made her angry. Maybe she was so angry that she sent those men to do what they did to you."

Ma needs a reason. I don't blame her. I need one, too.
Something to make sense of the senselessness, something
to hang the pain on.

"Okay Ma. I'll stop speaking to Nyasha. I won't be her
friend anymore."

It wasn't a complete lie. I hadn't heard from Nyasha since
the mincemeat incident, and I suspected that our friendship
had died with the alleged stabbing. I probably should have
called to apologize, but I was sick and I was dealing with my
own shit. Ma said she didn't think she was badly hurt. And
anyway, I was the one who was fucking raped, so if anybody
needed moral support it was me.

❖

When I got back to our flat that night, the "night of the
rape" as Dr. Phakama would insist I say, Nyasha said I
shouldn't tell people what had happened. She said it would
just give white people more ammunition, so they can scoff
at us and say, "You see, we told you your people are animals." She said the police would handle it, and I shouldn't
let the white doctors suck me into their self-pity. She said
our country was still growing and adjusting, and that these
things would settle with time. She said she was sorry for
what happened to me, but that I should rise above it and be
like the forefathers of the nation, who denied themselves
for a greater cause.

I remember being furious. Why couldn't Nyasha let go of her anger even for just a minute, when I, her friend, her sister, so badly needed her to put it aside and just hold me? Her hands were always so full of good arguments, unsettled debts, and old grudges that there was no room for anything else.

As usual I said nothing. I loved her and didn't want to let her down, or the cause, the country, the forefathers. And maybe I had just made it all up. Maybe I wasn't raped and was simply making excuses for the bad thing I was.

I was tired, and cooking after an overnight shift is never a good idea. But the lady at the pharmacy had said eating would help ease the ARV-associated nausea.

I'd written my prescription myself, the same script I'd written for so many women so many times that I could write it in my sleep. I needed to get on with the cooking now, but Nyasha kept on talking and talking and talking, explaining why the hatred between us South Africans and the rest of the continent was because of them, the white people. They had turned us against each other, and even at times like this we shouldn't let them win. As she talked and talked and the nausea grew and grew, I started to worry I might have mixed up my doses or even left something out. And still she kept talking. I heard her and then I didn't, and then my head started to hurt. Stop, I wanted to tell her. Stop, just fucking stop! I could smell my mincemeat smoldering on the stove, burning. It was making me want to vomit but

I couldn't get near it because there Nyasha was, in my way, talking and talking. If I did stab her, it was a mistake. I just wanted her to stop.

❖

You always think you'll feel it coming, but you don't. Maybe it's because people like claiming they'd known, had an ominous dream the day before, or felt a chill. I don't believe any of that. I think the day a bolt of lightning strikes you on your head is the day you're preoccupied with a piece of skin on your fingernail, a little piece hanging off your nail bed, a tiny juicy piece you just can't quite get a grip on with your teeth.

So you look back, you try to see if there were any signs, nudges. Maybe there were, or maybe you're just making them up as you go along, searching in places you know you never even walked past, lifting up couches, looking under rocks. It's a pointless exercise. Some things are completely out of our hands.

❖

Sometimes I forget. I get lost in the bassline of a song or the smell of lemongrass. At those times I'm just like everyone else. Then my mind asks, "Why are you so happy? Isn't there something you're forgetting?" And then I search and search and search, and I remember, oh yes, I was raped.

❖

I guess to some degree there's a sense of relief. I used to wonder what that thing would be for me—you know, that mountain, that valley, that shadow, that dark night of the soul. That bad thing that's waiting around the corner of everyone's life, the one that catches you off guard, collapses your world, shifts the ground beneath your feet. Ma used to say, "Don't be so negative. You mustn't think like that. Nothing is going to happen to you. Trust in God. You're just paranoid. Stop being silly. Are you premenstrual again?"

After Tshiamo's death I stopped worrying as much. I'd had my lot of suffering, I'd drunk my cup of pain, eaten my bitter share of heartache. I thought God would move on to others, at least for a little while.

But You have a reputation. So I decided that if suffering was to come my way again, I wouldn't allow it to be the end of me. If it was leukemia, I would write a best-selling memoir. If it was HIV, I'd become an activist. If I met my true love and he died on our wedding day, I'd take my twenty-one days of unused sick leave, cry my heart out in bed for three weeks, then get up and get back to it. Isn't that how one should approach it? Logically, rationally, sensibly. Because even if I try to convince You, negotiate, there are

no guarantees. There's no dose-related response; X number
of prayers does not equate to Y result. Nope, not with You,
none of that with You. After Tshiamo, I didn't think I'd be
defeated by loss again. I didn't think I could hurt any more
than I had. And I survived it, so surely there was nothing
more You could hurl at me that I couldn't handle? But as I
lay there on that floor, in that dark corridor, blood slowly
pooling around my pants, all I could think about was potas-
sium, 7.46 percent in the 10ml vial, 20 percent in the 20ml
vial and too little in the premixed solution to cause a fatal
arrhythmia.

❖

If anything, it's taught me humility. I think I had a big head.
I thought I was special, immune, exceptional. That these
sorts of things wouldn't happen to me. But I'm not. I'm
just another South African rape statistic. There's nothing
extraordinary about my story, it happens everywhere, every
day. It doesn't matter that I'm highly educated, a doctor,
that I started a petition that made the newspapers.

I have a vagina. That's all that matters.

❖

Some people say there were times in history when women
ruled the world. The same kind of people who claim that

there was a time when black people ruled the world. Fanciful nonsense. Even just physiologically, it's improbable that women ever lorded over men. Physical strength has always counted for more. The weight of a man on your chest, multiple men, one after another, empties your lungs. Even if your mind is sharper, with them on top no oxygen can reach your brain. It's impossible. Just try to picture a country ruled by the women I know. Ma, Nyasha, me. Ma rising and falling with the shadows, Nyasha cussing and swearing at history, and me: a bloody mess. It would be a joke.

❖

We went back to the police station this morning. They showed me the initial statement that was taken, and explained that they were still busy with the case. I wanted to tell them they'd written it all wrong. That the men didn't say, "Where are your friends now?" But that they said "Where are your *kwere-kwere* friends now?" I wanted to point out that it was my mouth they forced open, not my eyes, and that one first put his penis in my mouth and I had to suck it because I was scared. They left out that it felt like something was tearing inside. I'd told them that the second or third penis in my vagina grated like a fork against a brick, but they didn't write that down. The statement the officer had taken and reinterpreted was written on a page torn from an exercise book. Why did he use blue ink instead of black? At medical school I was taught that legal documents needed to be in black ink.

I should have corrected them. And I should have told them I thought one of the men was the same man who used to stand at the security box issuing keys for the doctors' rooms, and the other might be the voice on the switchboard, the voice that always sounded like it could see me from the other end of the line, that seemed to want to say more but didn't as it transferred me from Emergency Department to Surgery, to Outpatients. But the police station smelled of urine and the officer of drink, and I didn't want to upset Ma. So I said nothing.

The lawyer we saw later asked why none of my colleagues that morning noticed anything different about me. "Different like how?" I had asked him.

"If you've just been raped ma'am, you don't just go back to business as usual, and if you do, unless you're dead inside, there's something different about you."

Maybe I am dead inside. Or maybe I'm just pragmatic. You can't cry in the operating room. You can't let your unsterile teardrops fall into an open abdomen. And you can't cry between cases, either. The patients need drips, the blood results need to be fetched, preoperative medication needs prescribing. And even when you get home, you must shower, cook, eat, study, and try to get to bed early enough to bank up some sleep for the next day's call. When is there ever an opportunity to cry? You cry at church on Sunday if you're lucky enough to have the day off. Crying is a luxury we just don't have time for.

"Different like how? You think I'm making this up? Why would I make this up? You think I'm crazy?"

Ma said not to shout. The lawyer was just trying to get a clearer sense of the sequence of events. All of this was very confusing for everyone, and I mustn't get so angry. Nobody wants to hurt me. They just want to understand so they can help.

❖

As a doctor you learn to endure anything. How to plunge your fingers into a pus-filled vagina without scrunching up your nose. How to look a mother in the eye and lie to her about her baby dying inside. How to carefully wipe infected amniotic fluid off your face without gagging. You learn to work with difficult people, crazy people, dead people. You learn to stay up, and continue staying up. To shrug off criticism, and to eat your lunch in between dissecting cadavers. So as I lay there, I thought, okay, this is bad, this is really bad, but it will only last a few minutes, at most fifteen. That's it, fifteen minutes of your life. Just forget it ever happened, don't let fifteen minutes of your life haunt you forever.

❖

There's not much in this life one can count on to be there forever. Everything goes, everyone fades. There are peaks and valleys, then more peaks, but always more valleys. Some people call it exciting. They use words like "adventure." All I know is, I look forward to it coming to an end. Then, so I'm told, we all go to a place where everything stands still. Where all our favorite people are safe and happy and close by. Where we get to meet the most famous man in the world, who knows each of us by name, all our secrets, every hair on our heads, the smells we try to hide with perfume, the scars on our face that we cover with makeup, the dirt on our backs that we can't quite reach. And He loves us all the same, Father Joshua says. Loves us to death.

If only there was a way to skip through all this stuff and get to that place.

❖

When I see Tshiamo there, I'm going to slap him first before I kiss and hug him. Slap him first for all the heartache he's caused us by being so selfish and unkind. Slap him first for being a coward, for running away, for not thinking about us first, for only seeing himself and his own pain. But then I'll hug him and kiss him, because I miss him even now. I still miss him like it was only yesterday that he chose to leave us. I miss him even though I hate him for what he did.

❖

Tshiamo never liked me to touch him much. He never let me hold his hand, never even just let me rest my head against his shoulder. It didn't matter that I was really tired and my neck was sore. He said he didn't like it, it made him hot.

It hurt my feelings. It felt like he didn't love me. I wanted him to hold me, even just my hand. Sometimes, late at night, as we sat on the couch watching Friday night TV, I'd pretend to forget, to be fast asleep and not know what I was doing. But he'd still shrug my head off and inch away from me. I suppose he knew. He knew what he, what men, are capable of.

I used to think it might be because I smelled of blood, of off blood, like fish. I couldn't wait for Ma to let me use tampons so I wouldn't stink so bad. I thought maybe that was why Tshiamo didn't want me too near him.

❖

This morning I worked up the nerve to call the lab and ask for my results. The lady on the phone took a long time to find my name on the system. I had to spell it for her twice, and then give her my patient folder number. When she said, "Everything's fine," I didn't understand what her words meant initially.

"Everything's fine?" I asked, a little annoyed at the liberal use of the word "everything."

She said it again. "Everything's fine. Everything's normal. Sero-negative, as in, no HIV, *sisi*."

She was in a hurry. I was probably the umpteenth anxious clinician who'd called that day and she probably thought I was just another needlestick injury. But still. There was no need to be rude.

"Hello? Hello? Are you still there?"

"Yes, I am."

"Everything's fine. You're negative. There's been no seroconversion."

"Okay, thanks."

"But be more careful next time. We've had one or two come back positive this year. You doctors need to be more cautious."

Then she dropped the phone.

❖

Eight weeks to the day, today. Eight weeks to the day.

❖

I have no fight left in me. I've surrendered completely to the physics and the chemistry and the molecules of unanswered prayers that float above and past my head. I want nothing, and have accepted that nothing wants me. I am neither waiting, nor hoping. Neither disbelieving nor anticipating. I just am.

❖

The mornings are quiet here at home, nothing like at the hospital. There's no singing here. Ma wilted when Tshiamo died, like spinach in a little bit of heat. She moves without a sound, appears out of nowhere, sits for hours alone in the dark. There's no morning prayer in this place, no great amen. The house smells of nothing. No industrial bleach to purge the floors, no washbasins bubbling with scented soaps sent as gifts by visiting family, no bells to chase them home. There's nothing here.

❖

I miss it.

❖

I didn't think that I'd ever feel like this. That I'd actually miss it. The hospital, that is. Perhaps it's being so palpably useful that I miss, even if it's in the most useless ways. Perhaps it's touching people that I miss. Feeling pulses ten, twelve, twenty times a day. Thready pulses, bounding pulses, hammering pulses, fading pulses morning, noon, and night. Perhaps it's the smells: birth, death, soap, stool, coffee, alcohol, over and over again. It's the most real thing I know. The only real thing I know.

❖

We've been pretty broke these past few weeks—haven't paid the lights. I googled how long it takes before they switch them off, because data is something I still have. I feel guilty asking You for help, Lord, because I have a job, I can earn money. I'm just too scared to go back.

After five days of bereavement leave, I got an email warning that any additional time at home would be unpaid. Then, a few weeks later, a lady from Human Resources called to ask where I was.

"Does she know she has to finish her internship within three years of graduating? She'll have to rewrite her final year exams if she doesn't come back to work."

I heard Ma shouting at her over the phone. "What kind of person are you? Do you have any idea what she's been through?" Ma insisted that I'd return when I was ready. She said we didn't care if they stopped my salary.

Of course we cared.

❖

I had thought all the problems were out there: the hospital, the nurses, the CEO, the clerks, the lab, the blood bank, the porters, the security guards, the dietician, the physiotherapist, the OT, the specialists, the lazy registrars, the cats, the cleaners, the mice, the community, the MEC, the minister, the government, the president, the country, the world. I thought if I could just hide here, I'd be fine. But somehow the problems seem to have followed me home, to where I grew up, found a way into the bedroom I shared with Tshiamo when we were little and I didn't know that he was a boy and I was a girl.

❖

"Chaba, are you going to let those bastards win?" Nyasha would say. "Get up, wash your face, and let's get back to the business of our lives." Or "Chaba, when last did you bath? You smell like shit! Get up, let's go find those scumbags and fuck them up." Or "Chaba, turn this thing around. Don't be a victim, be a victor!" Or some lame crap like that. You know *mos* Nyasha, Lord. That's all she's good for. Talk, talk, talk. Where is she now?

If it wasn't for her, none of this would ever have happened.

❖

Ma asked me to go to Hillside Shopping Center with her this morning. There was no food in the fridge and no money in either of our purses, but there was still petrol in the car. I think she wanted to see what we could get with the nothing that we had.

As we walked into the mall, we saw a R200 note on the floor. I'd noticed the white lady in front of us digging in her bag, and it most likely fell out of there. But the speed with which Ma picked it up and slipped it into her pocket shut my mouth.

I knew Ma had seen the white lady, too. I knew she knew. So when she said, "It's our lucky day!" I just smiled and nodded. Ma doesn't believe in luck. Pagans believe in luck. Ma believes in God, *Badimo*, blessings, and miracles.

I feel guilty that I've brought us to this place, where Ma—church-going, ancestor-revering, scripture-quoting Ma—is reduced to stealing.

I have to go back to work.

❖

But what if I can't remember anything? What if someone asks who I am? What if they want to know where I've been? What if there's a cardiac arrest and I have to do something? What if I can't move, can't speak, can't think? What if I start to bleed? What if the men hear I'm there and come back for me?

What if I mess up my second chance?

❖

It's 5 a.m.

Right now the night-shift nurses are waking up, switching on lights, switching off heaters. Packing back the chairs they used as beds. Patients are stirring. Cell phone alarms are going off in the pockets of doctors—the young and naive ones, who thought there might be an opportunity to sleep on a Friday night call, to sleep so much that an alarm would need to be set. Mothers who have delivered babies in the night are being marched downstairs to the overflow ward, so their bloodstained sheets can be cleaned for the next batch of moms-to-be waiting anxiously on the benches as their babies struggle to free themselves from within. Statistics of the night's activities are being written up, estimated, changed. The bodies of those who slipped away in the night are being wrapped in plastic. Porters are scrambling for stretchers to wheel them off to the mortuary before the matrons and specialists arrive for their morning rounds. The security guard at the gate is whistling.

It's a new day.

❖

I can't lie here forever. I have to get up and move past this. It's done. There's no point kneading it any further.

Part 4

You are my God; apart from You I have no good thing.

Psalm 16:2

I felt a beating in my stomach, as though my heart had grown so weary it had sunk to the pit of my thorax. It turns out that the sporadic thuds I'd been feeling came from the body of another, a little baby, living, growing, thriving in the darkness.

❖

After the rape, my periods were all over the place, like they'd always been. I suppose it was more spotting than bleeding. But what did I care at the time about some vaginal bleeding? It wasn't like it was something I'd never experienced before. And anyway, I had bigger fish to fry. I'd just been raped. In those first few weeks, who could tell if it was the ARVs or the antipsychotics that made me vomit so?

Nobody dared rouse me from my bed. I paid no mind to my lack of energy, lack of appetite, the urge to retch at the sight of Jungle Oats. What difference did it make? What difference did anything make? I only wanted to be dead.

I am a doctor. I should have thought, should have suspected, even expected, that I might be expecting. But I didn't. I didn't think You could be so cruel.

It never occurred to me that I could be pregnant, until she moved like a heartbeat in my tummy.

❖

I suppose pregnancy had never really been in the picture for me after all the procedures I'd had to calm my raging uterus. In fact, one outraged doctor, who couldn't believe I'd been given an endometrial ablation so young, had told me that getting pregnant was both unlikely and dangerous.

So when I saw her there on the screen at that first ultrasound—her heart pulsing at 140 beats per minute, her body perfectly formed, her thumb in her mouth—I didn't believe them. Didn't believe the sonographer and her student who was smiling from ear to ear and wanting to give me a congratulatory hug.

A *baby*? I was going to have a baby?

I could tell Ma was in disbelief, too, because she said nothing all the way home. They gave us printouts of the ultrasound scans, and cards with appointment dates for all manner of investigations, but for the weeks that followed they remained on the dashboard of the car, untouched, just as we'd left them on that first drive back from the hospital.

❖

Our medical aid was suspended due to non-payment, so I had to give birth at Amogelang Regional Hospital. I was petrified, of course. I expected the worst: a large swig of my own bitter medicine. Instead I was under the care of a kind man with a kind heart. He introduced himself as Dr. Haffejee, and looked like an angel sent from God as he sat by my bedside, taking a history in his white flowing thobe. He raised an eyebrow a little when I admitted that I hadn't attended antenatal care until the third trimester of pregnancy.

I explained that I didn't know, didn't think, hadn't realized it was even possible, because I'd bled so much, and had had an endometrial ablation in my late teens. He put a soft hand on my arm and said it was okay. It was so reassuring, it made me weep.

I explained that the baby was conceived through sexual assault, that I was on call when it happened, and had been too scared to tell anyone, other than my roommate, who I then stabbed. So I was put on antipsychotics and antidepressants. I explained that I had prescribed the post-exposure prophylaxis myself, using a page in one of my patient's files, which I later tore out after the medication was dispensed. I was no longer sure whether I'd taken the morning-after pill, if I'd prescribed it or forgotten, or taken it and vomited it up, or taken it and it simply failed. I was too sick those first few days, mentally and physically. I could remember so little. So much still didn't make sense, and anyway, with no lining in my womb, was it even possible?

He said I shouldn't be so hard on myself, or feel guilty. As doctors we aren't trained to take care of ourselves, only to care for others. The system had failed me that night. Someone should have noticed. Someone should have picked up that I wasn't okay.

He said some bleeding in early pregnancy wasn't uncommon, even for a normal, healthy uterus, but with my history of endometrial ablation I was at greater risk of recurrent bleeds during pregnancy, and was fortunate to have carried successfully so far.

I wasn't sure if I agreed with the word "fortunate," but he was such a nice man, such a godly man, I didn't want to upset him with my ambivalence toward the new life that I would, in less than twenty-four hours, be bringing into the world.

He explained that they would have to deliver the baby early via cesarean section, due to the risk of uterine rupture. I had been added to the operating list for that evening. A nurse would soon be with me to prepare me for surgery, and all I needed to do was rest, relax, and let them take care of everything.

I don't remember feeling anything. Not in my body, not in my heart. Everything was numb—my toes, my legs, my soul. When the nurse handed her to me, I was afraid to look at her face. What if it was like the face of the one who bit my tongue, or the one who laughed when I started to cry . . . ?

But she looked like nothing, like a blank page, like a fresh start. My fresh start.

❖

I was happy she was light in complexion. At least God had given her that. Being dark on top of everything else (a child of rape) would have been too much.

But Ma had to take that away from us, too. She couldn't just be silent and enjoy the unexpected fairness of her complexion.

"You can see by the ears that she'll be as black as night. The ears always tell you the true complexion. The lightness won't last."

❖

I wondered which of the three was her father. The one who ejaculated before he could put his penis in, or the one who shouted, "Where are your *kwere-kwere* friends now?" Or maybe it was the one whose belly protruded beneath his striped T-shirt?

Or was it all of them? Is that possible? Could *all* of them be her father?

Is it possible that some goodness in them (because surely there's goodness in all of us?) came together to form her, despite their evil intentions, in spite of their evil intentions, to spite their evil intentions?

Is that possible?

❖

"Do not worry," I told her. "Don't you worry about a thing." I've spent my whole life worried. I worried in Grade One that I'd never be able to read. Then I worried I'd never make friends. Later I worried about bleeding to death. Not a day ever passed when I didn't worry. Would I ever learn to drive? Would I ever fall in love? Would a man ever love me? Would I ever be happy again?

When the midwife asked if there was anything I wanted to tell my baby before they took her to the neonatal ICU, I told her, "Don't worry. Don't worry about a thing."

❖

Will I tell her about her father(s)? I don't know. How do I explain the violence? That she was born of violation yet wanted still? That she was both the worst and the best thing to have happened to my life? That because of her conception I wanted to die, but that it was her life that forced me to live?

❖

I named her Mpho because that is what she is, because it's not her fault, because she doesn't deserve to have this stain on her future, because I refuse to allow anyone to tell her, or me, otherwise. She's my Mpho, my gift.

❖

I would have liked to introduce Mpho to Nyasha. She's a fighter, just like Nyasha. But after I went on maternity leave, Nyasha and I stopped speaking completely. Ma didn't invite Nyasha to the baby shower. And after the birth, well, I was just so busy, just so busy all the time. I guess I expected her to call, even text maybe. I wasn't angry. I understood that people didn't know how to react, whether to send congratulations or condolences. And then the time just went, cementing open the crack that had already split the ground between us.

When I went back to work after my maternity leave, Sister Agnes told me Nyasha had relocated to Canada. After qualifying she'd joined an agency and was doing locums there. The money was good and there was a chance she'd get a full-time position after doing some clinical time.

"*Canada?*"

"You know *mos* how hard it is for these foreigners here in South Africa, Doctor. I think all this xenophobia nonsense gets too much for them. Didn't she tell you?"

I couldn't hide my hurt, and Sister Agnes could see. A whole other country without even saying goodbye? Sister Agnes said I shouldn't be so hard on her, said we all knew how difficult it was for foreign doctors to get posts, that maybe she grew tired of South Africans accusing them of stealing their jobs.

"You know *mos* how things are, Doctor."

"Canada?"

"I'm sure she was just in a rush, Doctor. I'm sure she'll call you. Yoh, moving is hectic. And moving overseas! I remember when I moved to Saudi, in all that excitement, I didn't call my son for two weeks. My only son! Two weeks and I didn't phone him."

"But, Canada?"

"She will call, Doctor."

Nyasha is unbelievable. After everything, she leaves without saying goodbye? Not just to Nigeria or Kenya or even back home to Zim. But to an us-less place, where she will slip into the brain-drain statistics and live an anonymous life. Canada? All I know about Canada is that it gets so cold that when children wait outside for their school bus, their eyelashes freeze closed.

Why didn't she take a break if she was tired? Go on holiday to Canada and come back? Or if she was scared, why didn't she stay home for a couple of days, even weeks? Take unpaid leave. We all know this xenophobia thing will blow over. It won't last. Yes, from time to time there's an incident here and there, but it's definitely on the decline. Things are getting better.

Canada?

What will you find in a place where people don't hurt, don't suffer, don't fear, don't cry, don't die and rot? What will you discuss with people whose nails are clean and whose doors lie open as they sleep at night? How will you connect with so much sterility?

When I told Ma how Nyasha had left, how tired I was of people leaving me, everybody leaving me, nobody loving me enough to stay, Ma exclaimed, "Canada? *Aborehwaa*! Let her have her Canada! They deserve each other!"

Then the Nyasha stories kept coming. Everybody at work wanted to tell me about her. If it wasn't that she was in Canada, it was that she'd moved to the UK to be with her mother. Even the porters knew something about Nyasha's departure. It seemed she'd made time to say goodbye to everybody but me.

"That Dr. Nyasha, she was almost finished specializing, then this opportunity came and she decided to jump at it. You know these foreigners, Doctor. They don't mind starting from scratch if it'll get them ahead. They can start from scratch over and over again, they don't mind. As long as it'll get them ahead. Like Dr. Ogu, ne? Did you know he was a professor in his country? Why do you think he can do a bone marrow aspiration so fast? They are not like our children, these foreigners. Yoh, our children, Doctor, they are just waiting for the next contract. It's business idea after business idea, they are out having drinks Monday to Sunday, and they tell you it's called networking. They drive big cars, you don't even know where the money comes from. If in the next ten years they tell us the president of the ANC is a Nigerian, you know, I wouldn't be surprised, Doctor. We are sitting on our hands, us South Africans! Ah! *Wena*, you just wait and see."

❖

Even long after Nyasha walked out of my life, got on a plane and disappeared like we'd never existed, I still dreamed of her, thought I spotted her in malls, parking lots, traffic jams. I wonder what she'd say if she saw me now, as a mother. Sometimes I still seek her approval as I dress, plan, dream.

But she never loved me, Nyasha. Not like I loved her. I was always too South African, too Christian, too Westernized, too brainwashed, too weak, too afraid for the big thing she was.

❖

Sometimes I think it might have been better for Mpho to have stayed in the womb. In there she could tumble and spin, lick her fingers and rub her eyes and not worry about failure, disease, disappointment, heartbreak, loneliness, and unanswered prayers. In there she was safe and perfectly protected.

But she had to come out. Even that safe place would have turned against her after nine months, turned into hard, hostile rock. She had to come out, as we all did. To face what we all have to face.

❖

Sometimes at work, someone who has heard will work up the courage to ask how I'm coping with what's happened. Some really try to be sympathetic, but others are only trying to comfort their own fears. They ask me questions like why the security guards didn't come to my aid that night, or whether I think the "attack" was related to the petition I started. It's not me they're worried about, it's themselves. They want to be reassured that there was something unique about me—my story, my poor choices—that landed me in this situation. They want me to soothe them. "No, it was my fault," they want to hear, so they can feel safe from the same fate.

I've grown a little bit; I'm empathetic to their fears, so I tell them the lies they want to hear so they'll leave me alone. Leave me to go home and be with my Mpho.

She's beautiful, Mpho. Sometimes I find myself losing whole hours of a day because of all the time I spend just staring at her. Staring at her for no reason at all, other than

just that she's so painfully beautiful. Those big, loving, for-
giving, shiny black eyes. That toothless smile. I don't think
I've ever known anything like her in my life.

I don't even write in this journal as much as I used to.
I don't need to, I suppose. For once in my life, my heart is
still.

I asked Ma how something so perfect, so magnificent,
could come from so much darkness. Ma said it's because
Mpho is like those flowers, those nighttime flowers that only
bloom when the sun is long forgotten, like the evening primrose with all its healing powers.

Sometimes Ma can be so annoying, but sometimes she
says the nicest things.

❖

Today I am taking Mpho to get her immunizations. This
morning she woke up all smiles, laughing and cooing.
When I sang to her she kicked her arms and legs in delight.
She hasn't a care in the world. But I've been carrying her
around all morning with a heaviness in my heart, nervous
about the pain the nurse will inflict on her later in the
day. A necessary pain. One that will save her, protect her,
spare her from suffering in the future. One day she'll thank
me. But I feel bad nevertheless. No mother can bear to
watch her child get hurt. As she happily bats at the little
creatures hanging from her playpen, I prepare her diaper

bag for the clinic visit. I dress appropriately. My shirt has buttons that slip open easily, so I can soothe her at the breast after the injections. I pack a change of clothes for her in case, like last time, she cries so frantically that she brings up her breakfast.

If I was to explain to her what awaits her, she would not understand. She is too young, and, anyway, to what end? The deed must be done, the jab must be given. Why spoil her morning with stressful information, when I will be right there by her side to comfort her when it is all over?

About the Type

Typeset in Sabon MT at 11.5/15 pt.

Sabon's creator, Jan Tschichold, was commissioned in 1964 to create a typeface 5 percent narrower than Monotype Garamond that could be printed identically on Linotype, Monotype, or letterpress equipment. The new typeface was named for Jacques Sabon, who had played a role in bringing Garamond's type into use in German printing in the sixteenth century.

Typeset by Scribe Inc., Philadelphia, Pennsylvania.